"You can't just. . . **weeks on end be** **deal to complete**

"Incendiary words, Miss .... Lucas leaned over and placed both hands on either side of her chair, caging her in so that she automatically cringed back. The power of his personality was so suffocating that she had to make an effort to remember how to breathe. "I won't be kidnapping you. Far from it. You can walk out of here, but you know the consequences of that if you do. I am an extremely powerful man, for my sins. Please do us both a favor by not crossing me."

"Arrogant." Katy's green eyes narrowed in a display of bravado she was inwardly far from feeling. "That's what you are, Mr. Cipriani! You're an arrogant, domineering bully!" She collided with eyes that burned with the heat of molten lava.

Lucas's eyes drifted to her full lips and for a second he was overwhelmed by a powerful, crazy urge to crush them under his mouth. He drew back, straightened and resumed his seat behind his desk.

"I can't just be *kept under watch* for *two weeks*. How is it going to work?"

"It's simple." He leaned forward, the very essence of practicality. "You will be accommodated without benefit of your phone or personal computer for a fortnight. You can consider it a pleasant holiday without the nuisance of having your time interrupted by gadgets."

"A pleasant holiday?" Her breathing was ragged and her imagination, released to run wild, was coming up with all sorts of giddying scenarios...

Cathy Williams can remember reading Harlequin books as a teenager, and now that she is writing them, she remains an avid fan. For her, there is nothing like creating romantic stories and engaging plots, and each and every book is a new adventure. Cathy lives in London, and her three daughters—Charlotte, Olivia and Emma—have always been, and continue to be, the greatest inspirations in her life.

Books by Cathy Williams

Harlequin Presents

The Italian Titans

One Night With Consequences

Seven Sexy Sins

Visit the Author Profile page at Harlequin.com for more titles.

Cathy Williams

CIPRIANI'S INNOCENT CAPTIVE

ISBN-13: 978-0-373-21367-2

Cipriani's Innocent Captive

First North American Publication 2017

Copyright © 2017 by Cathy Williams

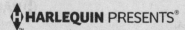

Recycling programs
for this product may
not exist in your area.

ISBN-13: 978-0-373-21367-2

Cipriani's Innocent Captive

First North American Publication 2017

Copyright © 2017 by Cathy Williams

Printed in U.S.A.

www.Harlequin.com

CIPRIANI'S INNOCENT CAPTIVE

CHAPTER ONE

'MR CIPRIANI IS ready for you now.'

Katy Brennan looked up at the middle-aged, angular woman who had earlier met her in the foyer of Cipriani Head Office and ushered her to the directors' floor, where she had now been waiting for over twenty minutes.

She didn't want to feel nervous but she did. She had been summoned from her office in Shoreditch, where she worked as an IT specialist in a small team of four, and informed that Lucas Cipriani, the ultimate god to whom everyone answered, requested her presence.

She had no idea why he might want to talk to her, but she suspected that it concerned the complex job she was currently working on and, whilst she told herself that he probably only wanted to go through some of the finer details with her, she was still...*nervous*.

Katy stood up, wishing that she had had

some kind of advance warning of this meeting, because if she had she would have dressed in something more in keeping with the über-plush surroundings in which she now found herself.

As it was, she was in her usual casual uniform of jeans and a tee-shirt, with her backpack and a lightweight bomber jacket, perfect for the cool spring weather, but utterly inappropriate for this high-tech, eight-storey glasshouse.

She took a deep breath and looked neither left nor right as she followed his PA along the carpeted corridor, past the hushed offices of executives and the many boardrooms where deals worth millions were closed, until the corridor ballooned out into a seating area. At the back of this was a closed eight-foot wooden door which was enough to send a chill through any person who had been arbitrarily summoned by the head of her company—a man whose ability to make deals and turn straw into gold was legendary.

Katy took a deep breath and stood back as his PA pushed open the door.

Staring absently through the floor-to-ceiling pane of reinforced glass that separated him from the streets below, Lucas Cipriani thought that this meeting was the last thing he needed to kick off the day.

But it could not be avoided. Security had been breached on the deal he had been working on for the past eight months, and this woman was going to have to take the consequences— pure and simple.

This was the deal of a lifetime and there was no way he was going to allow it to be jeopardised.

As his PA knocked and entered his office, Lucas slowly turned round, hand in trouser pocket, and looked at the woman whose job was a thing of the past, if only she knew it.

Eyes narrowed, it hit him that he really should catch up on the people who actually worked for him, because he hadn't expected this. He'd expected a nerd with heavy spectacles and an earnest manner, whilst the girl in front of him looked less like a computer whizz-kid and more like a hippy. Her clothes were generic: faded jeans and a tee-shirt with the name of a band he had never heard of. Her shoes were masculine black boots, suitable for heavy-duty construction work. She had a backpack slung over her shoulder, and stuffed into the top of it was some kind of jacket, which she had clearly just removed. Her entire dress code contradicted every single thing he associated with a woman, but she had the sort of multi-coloured coppery hair that would have had artists queuing up to commit it to canvas, and an elfin face with enormous bright-green eyes that held his gaze for reasons he couldn't begin to fathom.

'Miss Brennan.' He strolled towards his desk as Vicky, his secretary, clicked the heavy door to his office shut behind her. 'Sit, please.'

At the sound of that deep, dark, velvety voice, Katy started and realised that she had been holding her breath. When she had entered the office she'd thought that she more or less knew what to expect. She vaguely knew what her boss looked like because she had seen pictures of him in the company magazines that occasionally landed on her desk in Shoreditch, far away from the cutting-edge glass building that housed the great and the good in the company: from Lucas Cipriani, who sat at the very top like a god atop Mount Olympus, to his team of powerful executives who made sure that his empire ran without a hitch.

Those were people whose names appeared

on letterheads and whose voices were occasionally heard down the end of phone lines, but who were never, ever seen. At least, not in Shoreditch, which was reserved for the small cogs in the machine.

But she still hadn't expected *this*. Lucas Cipriani was, simply put, beautiful. There was no other word to describe him. It wasn't just the arrangement of perfect features, or the burnished bronze of his skin, or even the dramatic masculinity of his physique: Lucas Cipriani's good looks went far beyond the physical. He exuded a certain power and charisma that made the breath catch in your throat and scrambled your ability to think in straight lines.

Which was why Katy was here now, in his office, drawing a blank where her thoughts should be and with her mouth so dry that she wouldn't have been able to say a word if she'd wanted to.

She vaguely recalled him saying something about sitting down, which she badly wanted to do, and she shuffled her way to the enormous leather chair that faced his desk and sank into it with some relief.

'You've been working on the Chinese deal,' Lucas stated without preamble.

'Yes.' She could talk about work, she could answer any question he might have, but she was unsettled by a dark, brooding, in-your-face sensuality she hadn't expected, and when she spoke her voice was jerky and nervous. 'I've been working on the legal side of the deal, dedicating all the details to a programme that will enable instant access to whatever is required, without having to sift through reams of documentation. I hope there isn't a problem. I'm running ahead of schedule, in actual fact. I'll be honest with you, Mr Cipriani, it's one of the most exciting projects I've ever worked on. Complex, but really challenging.'

She cleared her throat and hazarded a smile, which was met with stony silence, and her already frayed nerves took a further battering. Stunning dark eyes, fringed with inky black, luxuriant lashes, pierced through the thin veneer of her self-confidence, leaving her breathless and red-faced.

Lucas positioned himself at his desk, an enormous chrome-and-glass affair that housed a computer with an over-sized screen, a metallic lamp and a small, very artfully designed bank of clocks that made sure he knew, at any given moment, what time it was in all the major cities in which his companies were located.

He lowered his eyes now and, saying nothing, swivelled his computer so that it was facing her.

'Recognise that man?'

Katy blanched. Her mouth fell open as she found herself staring at Duncan Powell, the guy she had fallen for three years previously. Floppy blond hair, blue eyes that crinkled when he grinned and boyish charm had combined to hook an innocent young girl barely out of her teens.

She had not expected this. Not in a million years. Confused, flustered and with a thousand alarm bells suddenly ringing in her head, Katy fixed bewildered green eyes on Lucas.

'I don't understand…'

'I'm not asking you to understand. I'm asking you whether you know this man.'

'Y-yes,' she stammered. 'I… Well, I knew him a few years ago…'

'And it would seem that you bypassed certain security systems and discovered that he is, these days, employed by the Chinese company I am in the process of finalising a deal with. Correct? No, don't bother answering that. I have a series of alerts on my computer and what I'm saying does not require verification.'

She felt dazed. Katy's thoughts had zoomed back in time to her disastrous relationship with Duncan.

She'd met him shortly after she had returned home to her parents' house in Yorkshire. Torn between staying where she was and facing the big, brave world of London, where the lights were bright and the job prospects were decidedly better, she had taken up a temporary post as an assistant teacher at one of the local schools to give herself some thinking time and to plan a strategy.

Duncan had worked at the bank on the high street, a stone's throw from the primary school.

In fairness, it had not been love at first sight. She had always liked a quirky guy; Duncan had been just the opposite. A snappy dresser, he had homed in on her with the single-minded focus of a heat-seeking missile with a pre-set target. Before she'd even decided whether she liked him or not, they had had coffee, then a meal, and then they were going out.

He'd been persistent and funny, and she'd started rethinking her London agenda when the whole thing had fallen apart because she'd discovered that the man who had stolen her heart wasn't the honest, sincere, single guy he had made himself out to be.

Nor had he even been a permanent resident in the little village where her parents lived. He'd been there on a one-year secondment, which was a minor detail he had cleverly kept under wraps. He had a wife and twin daughters keeping the fires warm in the house in Milton Keynes he shared with them.

She had been a diversion and, once she had discovered the truth about him, he had shrugged and held his hands up in rueful surrender and she had known, in a flash of pure gut instinct, that he had done that because she had refused to sleep with him. Duncan Powell had planned to have fun on his year out and, whilst he had been content to chase her for a few months, he hadn't been prepared to take the chase to a church and up an aisle, because he had been a fully committed family man.

'I don't understand.' Katy looked away from the reminder of her steep learning curve staring out at her from Lucas's computer screen. 'So Duncan works for their company. I honestly didn't go hunting for that information.'

Although, she *had* done some basic background checks, just out of sheer curiosity, to see whether it was the same creep once she'd stumbled upon him. A couple of clicks of a button was all it had taken to confirm her suspicion.

Lucas leaned forward, his body language darkly, dangerously menacing. 'That's as may be,' he told her, 'but it does present certain problems.'

With cool, clear precision he presented those *certain problems* to her and she listened to him in ever-increasing alarm. A deal done in complete secrecy…a family company rooted in strong values of tradition…a variable stock market that hinged on nothing being leaked and the threat her connection to Duncan posed at a delicate time in the negotiations.

Katy was brilliant with computers, but the mysteries of high finance were lost on her. The race for money had never interested her. From an early age, her parents had impressed upon her the importance of recognising value in the things that money couldn't buy. Her father was a parish priest and both her parents lived a life that was rooted in the fundamental importance of putting the needs of other people first. Katy didn't care who earned what or how much money anyone had. She had been brought up with a different set of values. For better or for worse, she occasionally thought.

'I don't care about any of that,' she said unevenly, when there was a brief lull in his cold tabulation of her transgressions. It seemed a good moment to set him straight because she was beginning to have a nasty feeling that he was circling her like a predator, preparing to attack.

Was he going to sack her? She would survive. The bottom line was that that was the very worst he could do. He wasn't some kind of mediaeval war lord who could have her hung, drawn and quartered because she'd disobeyed him.

'Whether you care about a deal that isn't going to impact on you or not is immaterial. Either by design or incompetence, you're now in possession of information that could unravel nearly a year and a half of intense negotiation.'

'To start with, I'm obviously very sorry about what happened. It's been a very complex job and, if I accidentally happened upon information I shouldn't have, then I apologise. I didn't mean to. In fact, I'm not at all interested in your deal, Mr Cipriani. You gave me a job to do and I was doing it to the best of my ability.'

'Which clearly wasn't up to the promised standard, because an error of the magnitude of the one you made is inexcusable.'

'But that's not fair!'

'Remind me to give you a life lesson about what's fair and what isn't. I'm not interested in your excuses, Miss Brennan. I'm interested in working out a solution to bypass the headache you created.'

Katy's mind had stung at his criticism of her ability. She was good at what she did. Brilliant, even. To have her competence called into question attacked the very heart of her.

'If you look at the quality of what I've done, sir, you'll find that I've done an excellent job. I realise that I may have stumbled upon information that should have not been available to me, but you have my word that anything I've uncovered stays right here with me.'

'And I'm to believe you because…?'

'Because I'm telling you the truth!'

'I'm sorry to drag you into the world of reality, Miss Brennan, but taking things at face value, including other people's *sincerely meant promises*, is something I don't do.' He leaned back into his chair and looked at her.

Without trying, Lucas was capable of exuding the sort of lethal cool that made grown men quake in their shoes. A chit of a girl who was destined for the scrapheap should have been a breeze but for some reason he was finding some of his formidable focus diluted by her arresting good looks.

He went for tall, career-driven brunettes who were rarely seen without their armour of high-end designer suits and killer heels. He enjoyed the back and forth of intellectual repartee and had oftentimes found himself embroiled in heated debates about work-related issues.

His women knew the difference between a bear market and a bull market and would have sneered at anyone who didn't.

They were alpha females and that was the way he liked it.

He had seen the damage caused to rich men by airheads and bimbos. His fun-loving, amiable father had had ten good years of marriage to Lucas's mother and then, when Annabel Cipriani had died, he had promptly lost himself in a succession of stunningly sexy blondes, intelligence not a prerequisite.

He had been taken to the cleaners three times and it was a miracle that any family money, of which there had been a considerable sum at the starting block, had been left in the coffers.

But far worse than the nuisance of having his bank accounts bled by rapacious golddiggers was the *hope* his father stupidly had always invested in the women he ended up marrying. Hope that they would be there for him, would somehow give him the emotional support he had had with his first wife. He had been looking for love and that weakness had opened him up to being used over and over again.

Lucas had absorbed all this from the side lines and had learned the necessary lessons: avoid emotional investment and you'd never end up getting hurt. Indeed, bimbos he could handle, though they repulsed him. At least they were a known quantity. What he really didn't do were women who demanded anything from him he knew he was incapable of giving, which was why he always went for women as emotionally and financially independent as him.

They obeyed the same rules that he did and were as dismissive of emotional, overblown scenes as he was.

The fact was that, if you didn't let anyone in, then you were protected from disappointment, and not just the superficial disappointment of discovering that some replaceable woman was more interested in your bank account than she was in *you*.

He had learned more valuable lessons about the sort of weaknesses that could permanently scar and so he had locked his heart away and thrown away the key and, in truth, he had never had a moment's doubt that he had done the right thing.

'Are you still in contact with the man?' he murmured, watching her like a hawk.

'No! I am *not*!' Heated colour made her face burn. She found that she was gripping the arms of the chair for dear life, her whole body rigid with affront that he would even ask her such a personal question. 'Are you going to sack me, Mr Cipriani? Because, if you are, then perhaps you could just get on with it.'

Her temples were beginning to throb painfully. Of course she was going to be sacked. This wasn't going to be a ticking off before being dismissed back to Shoreditch to resume her duties as normal, nor was she simply going to be removed from the task at which inadvertently she had blundered.

She had been hauled in here like a common criminal so that she could be fired. No one-month's notice, no final warning, and there was no way that she could even consider a plea of unfair dismissal. She would be left without her main source of income and that was something she would just have to deal with.

And the guy sitting in front of her having fun being judge, jury and executioner didn't give a hoot as to whether she was telling the truth or not, or whether her life would be affected by an abrupt sacking or not.

'Regrettably, it's not quite so straightforward—'

'Why not?' Katy interrupted feverishly. 'You obviously don't believe a word I've told you and I know I certainly wouldn't be allowed anywhere near the project again. If you just wanted me off it, you would have probably told Tim, my manager, and let him pass the message on to me. The fact that I've been summoned here tells me that you're going to give me the boot, but not before you make sure I know why. Will you at the very least give me a reference, Mr Cipriani? I've worked extremely hard for your company for the past year and a half and I've had nothing but glowing reports on the work I've done. I think I deserve some credit for that.'

Lucas marvelled that she could think, for a minute, that he had so much time on his hands that he would personally call her in just to sack her. She was looking at him with an urgent expression, her green eyes defiant.

Again distracted, he found himself saying, 'I noticed on your file that you only work two days a week for my company. Why is that?'

'Sorry?' Katy's eyes narrowed suspiciously.

'It's unusual for someone of your age to be a part-time employee. That's generally the domain of women with children of school age who want to earn a little money but can't afford the demands of a full-time job.'

'I...I have another job,' she admitted, wondering where this was heading and whether she needed to be on her guard. 'I work as an IT teacher at one of the secondary schools near where I live.'

Lucas was reluctantly fascinated by the ebb and flow of colour that stained her cheeks. Her face was as transparent as glass and that in itself was an unusual enough quality to hold his attention. The tough career women he dated knew how to school their expressions because, the higher up the ladder they climbed, the faster they learned that blushing like virginal maidens did nothing when it came to career advancement.

'Can't pay well,' he murmured.

'That's not the point!'

Lucas had turned his attention to his computer and was very quickly pulling up the file he had on her, which he had only briefly scanned before he had scheduled his meeting with her. The list of favourable references was impressively long.

'So,' he mused, sitting back and giving her his undivided attention. 'You work for me for the pay and you work as a teacher for the enjoyment.'

'That's right.' She was disconcerted at how quickly he had reached the right conclusions.

'So the loss of your job at my company would presumably have a serious impact on your finances.'

'I would find another job to take its place.'

'Look around the market, Miss Brennan.

Well paid part-time work is thin on the ground. I make it my duty to pay my employees over the odds. I find that tends to engender commitment and loyalty to the company. You'd be hard pressed to find the equivalent anywhere in London.'

Lucas had planned on a simple solution to this unexpected problem. Now, he was pressed to find out a bit more about her. As a part-time worker, it seemed she contributed beyond the call of duty, and both the people she answered to within the company and external clients couldn't praise her enough. She'd pleaded her innocence, and he wasn't gullible enough to wipe the slate clean, but a more detailed hearing might be in order. His initial impressions weren't of a thief who might be attracted to the lure of insider trading but, on the other hand, someone with a part-time job might find it irresistible to take advantage of an unexpected opportunity, and Duncan Powell represented that unexpected opportunity.

'Money doesn't mean that much to me, Mr Cipriani.' Katy was confused as to how a man whose values were so different from hers could make her go hot and cold and draw her attention in a way that left her feeling helpless and exposed. She was finding it hard to string simple sentences together. 'I have a place to myself but, if I had to share with other people, then it wouldn't be the end of the world.'

The thought of sharing space with a bunch of strangers was only slightly less appalling to Lucas than incarceration with the key thrown away.

Besides, how much did she mean that? he wondered with grim practicality, dark eyes drifting over her full, stubborn mouth and challenging angle of her head. What had been behind that situation with Powell, a married man? It wasn't often that Lucas found himself questioning his own judgements but in this instance he did wonder whether it was just a simple tale of a woman who had been prepared to overlook the fact that her lover was a married man because of the financial benefits he could bring to the table. Although, he'd seen enough of that to know that it was the oldest story in the world.

Maybe he would test the waters and see what came out in the wash. If this had been a case of hire and fire, then she would have been clearing out her desk eighteen hours ago, but it wasn't, because he couldn't sack her just yet, and it paid to know your quarry. He would not allow any misjudgements to wreck his deal.

'You never thought about packing in the teaching and taking up the job at my company full time?'

'No.' The silence stretched between them while Katy frantically tried to work out where this sudden interest was leading. 'Some people aren't motivated by money.' She finally broke the silence because she was beginning to perspire with discomfort. 'I wasn't raised to put any value on material things.'

'Interesting. Unique.'

'Maybe in *your* world, Mr Cipriani.'

'Money, Miss Brennan, is the engine that makes everything go, and not just in my world. In everyone's world. The best things in life are not, as rumour would have it, free.'

'Maybe not for you,' Katy said with frank disapproval. She knew that she was treading on thin ice. She sensed that Lucas Cipriani was not a man who enjoyed other people airing too many contradictory opinions. He'd hauled her in to sack her and was now subjecting her to the Spanish Inquisition because he was cold, arrogant and because *he could*.

But what was the point of tiptoeing around

him when she was on her way out for a crime she hadn't committed?

'That's why you don't believe what I'm saying,' she expanded. 'That's why you don't trust me. You probably don't trust anyone, which is sad, when you think about it. I'd hate to go through life never knowing my friends from my enemies. When your whole world is about money, then you lose sight of the things that really matter.'

Lucas's lips thinned disapprovingly at her directness. She was right when she said that he didn't trust anyone but that was exactly the way he liked it.

'Let me be perfectly clear with you, Miss Brennan.' He leaned forward and looked at her coolly. 'You haven't been brought here for a candid exchange of views. I appreciate you are probably tense and nervous, which is doubtless why you're cavalier about overstepping the mark, but I suggest it's time to get down from your moral high ground and take a long, hard look at the choices you have made that have landed you in my office.'

Katy flushed. 'I made a mistake with Duncan,' she muttered. 'We all make mistakes.'

'You slept with a married man,' Lucas corrected her bluntly, startling her with the revelation that he'd discovered what he clearly thought was the whole, shameful truth. 'So, while you're waxing lyrical about my tragic, money-orientated life, you might want to consider that, whatever the extent of my greed and arrogance, I would no more sleep with a married woman than I would jump into the ocean with anchors secured to my feet.'

'I...'

Lucas held up one hand. 'No one speaks to me the way you do.' He felt a twinge of discomfort because that one sentence seemed to prove the arrogance of which he had been accused. Since when had he become so *pompous*? He scowled. 'I've done the maths, Miss Brennan and, however much you look at me with those big, green eyes, I should tell you that taking the word of an adulterer is something of a tall order.'

Buffeted by Lucas's freezing contempt and outrageous accusations, Katy rose on shaky legs to direct the full force of her anger at him.

'How *dare you*?' But even in the midst of her anger she was swamped by the oddest sensation of vulnerability as his dark eyes swept

coolly over her, electrifying every inch of her
heated body.

'With remarkable ease.' Lucas didn't bat an
eyelid. 'I'm staring the facts in the face and
the facts are telling me a very clear story. You
want me to believe that you have nothing to
do with the man. Unfortunately, your lack of
principles in having anything to do with him
in the first place tells a tale of its own.'

The colour had drained away from her face.
She hated this man. She didn't think it would
be possible to hate anyone more.

'I don't have to stay here and listen to this.'
But uneasily she was aware that, without her
laying bare her sex life, understandably he
would have jumped to the wrong conclusions.
Without her confession that she had never slept
with Duncan, he would have assumed the obvious. Girls her age had flings and slept with
men. Maybe he would be persuaded into be-
lieving her if she told him the truth, which was
that she had ended their brief relationship as
soon as she had found out about his wife and
kids. But even if he believed that he certainly
wouldn't believe that she hadn't *slept* with the
man.

Which would lead to a whole other conversation and it was one she had no intention of having. How would a man like Lucas Cipriani believe that the hussy who slept with married guys was in fact a virgin?

Even Katy didn't like thinking about that. She had never had the urge to rush into sex. Her parents hadn't stamped their values on her but the drip, drip, drip of their gentle advice, and the example she had seen on the doorstep of the vicarage of broken-hearted, often pregnant young girls abandoned by men they had fallen for, had made her realise that when it came to love it paid to be careful.

In fairness, had temptation knocked on the door, then perhaps she might have questioned her old-fashioned take on sex but, whilst she had always got along just fine with the opposite sex, no one had ever grabbed her attention until Duncan had come along with his charm, his overblown flattery and his *persistence*. She had been unsure of where her future lay, and in that brief window of uncertainty and apprehension he had burrowed in and stolen her heart. She had been ripe for the picking and his betrayal had been devastating.

Her virginity was a millstone now, a reminder of the biggest mistake she had ever made. Whilst she hoped that one day she would find the guy for her, she was resigned to the possibility that she might never do so, because somehow she was just out of sync with men and what they wanted.

They wanted sex, first and foremost. To get to the prince, you seemed to have to sleep with hundreds of frogs, and there was no way she would do that. The thought that she might have slept with *one* frog was bad enough.

So what would Lucas Cipriani make of her story?

She pictured the sneer on his face and shuddered.

Disturbed at the direction of her thoughts, she tilted her chin and looked at him with equal cool. 'I expect, after all this, I'm being given the sack and that Personnel will be in touch—so there can't be any reason for me to still be here. And you can't stop me leaving. You'll just have to trust me that I won't be saying anything to anyone about your deal.'

CHAPTER TWO

SHE DIDN'T GET FAR.

'You leave this office, Miss Brennan, and regrettably I will have to commence legal proceedings against you on the assumption that you have used insider information to adversely influence the outcome of my company's business dealings.'

Katy stopped and slowly turned to look at him.

His dark eyes were flat, hard and expressionless and he was looking right back at her with just the mildest of interest. His absolute calm was what informed her that he wasn't cracking some kind of sick joke at her expense.

Katy knew a lot about the workings of computers. She could create programs that no one else could and was downright gifted when it came to sorting out the nuts and bolts of intricate problems when those programs began to get a little temperamental. It was why she had been carefully headhunted by Lucas's company and why they'd so willingly accommodated her request for a part-time job only.

In the field of advanced technology, she was reasonably well-known.

She didn't, however, know a thing about law. What was he going on about? She didn't really understand what he was saying but she understood enough to know that it was a threat.

Lucas watched the colour flood her face. Her skin was satiny smooth and flawless. She had the burnished copper-coloured hair of a redhead, yet her creamy complexion was free of any corresponding freckles. The net result was an unusual, absurdly striking prettiness that was all the more dramatic because she seemed so unaware of it.

But then, his cynical brain told him, she was hardly a shrinking violet with no clue of her pulling power, because she *had* had an affair with a married guy with kids.

He wondered whether she thought that she could turn those wide, emerald-green eyes on him and get away scot-free.

If she did, then she had no idea with whom she was dealing. He'd had a lifetime's worth of training when it came to spotting women who felt that their looks were a passport to getting whatever they wanted. He'd spent his formative years watching them do their numbers on his father. This woman might not be an airhead like them, but she was still driven by the sort of emotionalism he steered well clear of.

'Of course—' he shrugged '—my deal would be blown sky-high out of the water, but have you any idea how much damage you would do to yourself in the process? Litigation is something that takes its time. Naturally, your services would be no longer required at my company and your pay would cease immediately. And then there would be the small question of your legal costs. Considerable.'

Her expression was easy to read and Lucas found that he was enjoying the show.

'That's—that's ridiculous,' Katy stuttered. 'You'd find out that I haven't been in touch with...with Duncan for years. In fact, since we broke up. Plus, you'd *also* find out that I haven't breathed a word about the Chinese deal to...well, to anybody.'

'I only have your word for it. Like I said, discovering whether you're telling the truth or not would take time, and all the while you would naturally be without a penny to your name, defending your reputation against the juggernaut of my company's legal department.'

'I have another job.'

'And we've already established that teaching won't pay the rent. And who knows how willing a school would be to employ someone with a potential criminal record?'

Katy flushed. Bit by bit, he was trapping her in a corner and, with a feeling of surrendering to the inexorable advance of a steamroller, she finally said, 'What do you want me to do?'

Lucas stood up and strolled towards the wall of glass that separated him from the city below, before turning to look at her thoughtfully.

'I told you that this was not a straightforward situation, Miss Brennan. I meant it. It isn't a simple case of throwing you out of my company when you can hurt me with privileged information.' He paced the enormous office, obliging her to follow his progress, and all the time she found herself thinking, *he's almost too beautiful to bear looking at*. He was very tall and very lean, and somehow the finely cut, expensive suit did little to conceal something raw and elemental in his physique.

She had to keep dragging her brain back to what he was telling her. She had to keep frowning so that she could give the appearance of not looking like a complete nitwit. She didn't like the man, but did he have this effect on *all* the women he met?

She wondered what sort of women he met anyway, and then chastised herself for losing the thread when her future was at stake.

'The deal is near completion and a fortnight at most should see a satisfactory conclusion. Now, let's just say that I believe you when you tell me that you haven't been gossiping with your boyfriend...'

'I told you that Duncan and I haven't spoken for years! And, for your information, we broke up because *I found out that he was married.* I'm not the sort of person who would ever dream of going out with a married guy—!'

Lucas stopped her in mid-speech. 'Not interested. All I'm interested in is how this situation is dealt with satisfactorily for me. As far as I am concerned, you could spend all your free time hopping in and out of beds with married men.'

Katy opened her mouth and then thought better of defending herself, because it wasn't going to get her anywhere. He seemed ready to hand down her sentence.

'It is imperative that any sensitive information you may have acquired is not shared, and the only way that that can be achieved is if you are incommunicado to the outside world. Ergo that is how it is going to be for the next fortnight, until my deal is concluded.'

'Sorry, Mr Cipriani, but I'm not following you.'

'Which bit, exactly, Miss Brennan, are you not following?'

'The *fortnight* bit. What are you talking about?'

'It's crystal clear, Miss Brennan. You're not going to be talking to anyone, and I mean *anyone,* for the next two weeks until I have all the signatures right where I want them, at which point you may or may not return to your desk in Shoreditch and we can both forget that this unfortunate business ever happened. Can I get any clearer than that? And by "incommunicado", I mean no mobile phone and no computer. To be blunt, you will be under watch until you can no longer be a danger to me.'

'But you can't be serious!'

'Do I look as though I'm doing a stand-up routine?'

No, he didn't. In fact, without her even realising it, he had been pacing the office in ever decreasing circles and he was now towering right in front of her; the last thing he resembled was a man doing a stand-up routine.

Indeed, he looked about as humorous as an executioner; she quailed inside.

Mentally, she added 'bully' to the growing list of things she loathed about him.

'Under watch? What does that even mean? You can't just…just *kidnap* me for weeks on end because you have a deal to complete! That's a crime!'

'Incendiary words, Miss Brennan.' He leaned over and placed both hands on either side of her chair, caging her in so that she automatically cringed back. The power of his personality was so suffocating that she had to make an effort to remember how to breathe. 'I won't be kidnapping you. Far from it. You can walk out of here, but you know the consequences of that if you do. The simple process of consulting a lawyer would start racking up bills you could ill afford, I'm sure. Not to mention the whiff of unemployability that would be attached to you at the end of the long-winded and costly business. I am an extremely powerful man, for my sins. Please do us both a favour by not crossing me.'

'Arrogant.' Katy's green eyes narrowed in a display of bravado she was inwardly far from feeling. 'That's what you are, Mr Cipriani! You're an arrogant, domineering bully!' She collided with eyes that burned with the heat of molten lava, and for a terrifying moment her anger was eclipsed by a dragging sensation that made her breathing sluggish and laborious.

Lucas's eyes drifted to her full lips and for a second he was overwhelmed by a powerful, crazy urge to crush them under his mouth. He drew back, straightened and resumed his seat behind his desk.

'I'm guessing that you're beginning to see sense,' he commented drily.

'It's not ethical,' Katy muttered under her breath. She eyed him with mutinous hostility.

'It's perfectly ethical, if a little unusual, but then again I've never been in the position of harbouring suspicions about the loyalties of any of my employees before. I pay them way above market price and that usually works. This is a first for me, Miss Brennan.'

'I can't just be *kept under watch* for *two weeks*. I'm not a specimen in a jam jar! Plus, I have responsibilities at the school!'

'And a simple phone call should sort that out. If you want, I can handle the call myself. You just need to inform them that personal circumstances will prevent you from attending for the next fortnight. Same goes for any relatives, boyfriends and random pets that might need sorting out.'

'I can't believe this is happening. How is it going to work?'

'It's simple.' He leaned forward, the very essence of practicality. 'You will be accommodated without benefit of your phone or personal computer for a fortnight. You can consider it a pleasant holiday without the nuisance of having your time interrupted by gadgets.'

'A *pleasant holiday*?' Her breathing was ragged and her imagination, released to run wild, was coming up with all sorts of giddying scenarios.

Lucas had the grace to flush before shrugging. 'I assure you that your accommodation will be of the highest quality. All you need bring with you are your clothes. You will be permitted to return to your house or flat, or wherever it is you live, so that you can pack what you need.'

'Where on earth will I be going? This is mad.'

'I've put the alternative on the table.' Lucas shrugged elegantly.

'But where will I be *put*?'

'To be decided. There are a number of options. Suffice to say that you won't need to bring winter gear.' In truth, he hadn't given this a great deal of thought. His plan had been to delegate to someone else the responsibility of babysitting the headache that had arisen.

Now, however, babysitting her himself was looking good.

Why send a boy to do a man's job? She was lippy, argumentative, stubborn, in short as unpredictable as a keg of dynamite, and he couldn't trust any of his guys to know how to handle her.

She was also dangerously pretty and had no qualms when it came to having fun with a married guy. She said otherwise, but the jury was out on that one.

Dangerously pretty, rebellious and lacking

in a moral compass was a recipe for disaster. Lucas looked at her with veiled, brooding speculation. He frankly couldn't think of anyone who would be able to handle this. He had planned to disappear for a week or so to consolidate the finer details of the deal, without fear of constant interruption, and this had become even more pressing since the breach in security. He could easily kill two birds with one stone, rather than delegating the job and then wasting his time wondering whether the task would go belly up.

'So, to cut to the chase, Miss Brennan...' He buzzed and was connected through to his PA. In a fog of sick confusion, and with the distinct feeling of being chucked into a tumble drier with the cycle turned to maximum spin, Katy was aware of him instructing the woman who had escorted her to his office to join them in fifteen minutes.

'Yes?' she said weakly.

'Vicky, my secretary, is going to accompany you back to...wherever you live...and she will supervise your immediate packing of clothes to take with you. Likewise, she will oversee whatever phone calls you feel you have to make to your friends. Needless to say, these will have to be cleared with her.'

'This is ridiculous. I feel as though I'm starring in a low-grade spy movie.'

'Don't be dramatic, Miss Brennan. I'm taking some simple precautions to safeguard my business interests. Carrying on; once you have your bags packed and you've made a couple of calls, you will be chauffeured back here.'

'Can I ask you something?'

'Feel free.'

'Are you always this…*cold*?'

'Are you always this outspoken?' Eyes as black as night clashed with emerald-green. Katy felt something shiver inside her and suddenly, inexplicably, she was aware of her body in a way she had never been in her life before. It felt heavy yet acutely sensitive, tingly and hot, aching as though her limbs had turned to lead.

Her mouth went dry and for a few seconds her mind actually went completely blank. 'I think that, if I have something to say, then why shouldn't I? As long as I'm not being offensive to anyone, we're all entitled to our opinions.' She paused and tilted her chin at a challenging angle. 'To answer your question.'

Lucas grunted. Not even the high-powered women who entered and exited his life made a habit of disagreeing with him, and they certainly never criticised. No one did.

'And to answer yours,' he said coolly, 'I'm cold when the occasion demands. You're not here on a social visit. You're here because a situation has arisen that requires to be dealt with and you're the root cause of the situation. Trust me, Miss Brennan, I'm the opposite of cold, given the right circumstances.'

And then he smiled, a long, slow, lazy smile and her senses shot into frantic overdrive. She licked her lips and her body stiffened as she leant forward in the chair, clutching the sides like a drowning person clutches a lifebelt.

That smile.

It seemed to insinuate into parts of her that she hadn't known existed, and it took a lot of effort actually to remember that the man was frankly insulting her and that sexy smile was not directed at her. Whoever he was thinking of—his current girlfriend, no doubt—had instigated that smile.

Were he to direct a smile at her, it would probably turn her to stone.

'So you stuff me away somewhere...' She

finally found her voice and thankfully sounded as composed as he did. 'On a two week *holiday*, probably with those bodyguards of yours who brought me from the office, where I won't be allowed to do anything at all because I'll be minus my mobile phone and minus my computer. And, when you're done with your deal, you might just pop back and collect me, provided I've survived the experience.'

Lucas clicked his tongue impatiently. 'There's no need to be so dramatic.' He raked his fingers through his hair and debated whether he should have taken a slightly different approach.

Nope. He had taken the only possible approach. It just so happened that he was dealing with someone whose feet were not planted on the ground the way his were.

'The bodyguards won't be there.'

'No, I suppose it would be a little *chancy* to stuff me away with men I don't know. Not that it'll make a scrap of difference whether your henchmen are male or female. I'll still be locked away like a prisoner in a cell with the key thrown away.'

Lucas inhaled deeply and slowly, and hung on to a temper that was never, ever lost. 'No henchmen,' he intoned through gritted teeth. 'You're going to be with me. I wouldn't trust anyone else to keep an eye on you.'

Not without being mauled to death in the process.

'With *you*?' Shot through with an electrifying awareness of him, her heart sped up, sending the blood pulsing hotly through her veins and making it difficult to catch her breath. *Trapped somewhere with him?* And yet the thought, which should have filled her with unremitting horror, kick-started a dark, insurgent curiosity that frankly terrified her.

'I have no intention of having any interaction with you at all. You will simply be my responsibility for a fortnight and I will make sure that no contact is made with any outside parties until the deal is signed, sealed and delivered. And please don't tell me the prospect of being without a mobile phone or computer for a handful of days amounts to nothing short of torture, an experience which you may or may not survive! It *is* possible to live without gadgets for a fortnight.'

'Could *you*?' But her rebellious mind was somewhere else, somewhere she felt it shouldn't be.

'This isn't about me. Bring whatever books you want, or embroidery, or whatever you might enjoy doing, and think about it positively as an unexpected time out for which you will continue to be paid. If you're finding it difficult to kick back and enjoy the experience, then you can always consider the alternative: litigation, legal bills and no job.'

Katy clenched her fists and wanted to say something back in retaliation, even though she was dimly aware of the fact that this was the last person on the planet she wanted to have a scrap with, and not just because he was a man who would have no trouble in making good on his threats. However, the door was opening and through the haze of her anger she heard herself being discussed in a low voice, as if she wasn't in the room at all.

'Right.'

She blinked and Lucas was staring down at her, hands shoved in his trouser pockets. Awkwardly she stood up and instinctively smiled politely at his secretary, who smiled back.

He'd rattled off a chain of events, but she'd only been half listening, and now she didn't honestly know what would happen next.

'I'll have to phone my mum and dad,' she

said a little numbly and Lucas inclined his head to one side with a frown.

'Of course.'

'I talk with them every evening.'

His frown deepened, because that seemed a little excessive for someone in her twenties. It didn't tally with the image of a raunchy young woman indulging in a steamy affair with a married man, not that the details of that were his business, unless the steamy affair was ongoing.

'And I don't have any pets.' She gathered her backpack from the ground and headed towards the door in the same daze that had begun settling over her the second his secretary had walked into the room.

'Miss Brennan...'

'Huh?' She blinked and looked up at him.

She was only five-three and wearing flats, so she had to crane her neck up. Her hair tumbled down her back in a riot of colour. Lucas was a big man and he felt as though he could fit her into his pocket. She was delicate, her features fine, her body slender under the oversized white shirt. Was that why he suddenly felt himself soften after the gruelling experience he had put her through? He had never in his life done anything that disturbed his conscience, had always acted fairly and decently towards other people. Yes, undeniably he could be ruthless, but never unjustly so. He felt a little guilty now.

'Don't get worked up about this.' His voice was clipped because this was as close as he was going to get to putting her mind at ease. By nature, he was distrustful, and certainly the situation in which he had encountered her showed all the hallmarks of being dangerous, as she only had to advertise what she knew to her ex. Yet something about her fuelled an unexpected response in him.

Her eyes, he noted as he stared down into them, were a beguiling mix of green and turquoise. 'This isn't a trial by torture. It's just the only way I can deal with a potential problem. You won't spend the fortnight suffering, nor is there any need to fear that I'm going to be following you around every waking moment like a bad conscience. Indeed, you will hardly notice my presence. I will be working all day and you'll be free to do as you like. Without the tools for communicating with the outside world, you can't get up to any mischief.'

'But I don't even know where I'm going!' Katy cried, latching on to that window of empathy before it vanished out of sight.

Lucas raised his eyebrows, and there was that smile again, although the empathy was still there and it was tinged with a certain amount of cool amusement. 'Consider it a surprise,' he murmured. 'A bit like winning the lottery which, incidentally, pretty much sums it up when you think about the alternative.' He nodded to his secretary and glanced at his watch. 'Two hours, Vicky. Think that will do it?'

'I think so.'

'In that case, I will see you both shortly. And, Miss Brennan...don't even think about doing a runner.'

Over the next hour and a half Katy experienced what it felt like to be kidnapped. Oh, he could call it what he liked, but she was going to be held prisoner. She was relieved of her mobile phone by Lucas's secretary, who was brisk but warm, and seemed to see nothing amiss in following her boss's high-handed instructions. It would be delivered to Lucas and held in safekeeping for her.

She packed a bunch of clothes, not knowing where she was going. Outside, it was still, but spring was making way for summer, so the clothes she crammed into her duffel bag were light, with one cardigan in case she ended up somewhere cold.

Although how would she know what the weather was up to when she would probably be locked in a room somewhere with views of the outside world through bars?

And yet, for all her frustration and downright *anger,* she could sort of see why he had reacted the way he had. Obviously the only thing that mattered to Lucas Cipriani was making money and closing deals. If this was to be the biggest deal of his career—and dipping his corporate toes into the Far East would be—then he would be more than happy to do what it took to safeguard his interest.

She was a dispensable little fish in the very big pond in which he was the marauding king of the water.

And the fact that she knew someone at the company he was about to take over, someone who was so far ignorant of what was going on, meant she had the power to pass on highly sensitive and potentially explosive information.

Lucas Cipriani, being the sort of man he was, would never believe that she had no on-going situation with Duncan Powell because he was suspicious, distrustful, power hungry, arrogant, and would happily feed her to the sharks if it suited him, because he was also ice-cold and utterly emotionless.

'Where am I being taken?' she asked Vicky as they stepped back into the chauffeur-driven car that had delivered her to her flat. 'Or am I going to find myself blindfolded before we get there?'

'To a field on the outskirts of London.' She smiled. 'Mr Cipriani has his own private mode of transport there. And, no, you won't be blind-folded for any of the journey.'

Katy subsided into silence and stared at the scenery passing by as the silent car left London and expertly took a route with which she was unfamiliar. She seldom left the capital un-less it was to take the train up to Yorkshire to see her parents and her friends who still lived in the area. She didn't own a car, so escaping London was rarely an option, although, on a couple of occasions, she *had* gone with Tim and some of the others to Brighton for a holiday, five of them crammed like sardines into his second-hand car.

She hadn't thought about the dynamics of being trapped in a room with just Lucas acting as gaoler outside, but now she did, and she felt that frightening, forbidding tingle again.

Would other people be around? Or would there just be the two of them?

She hated him. She loathed his arrogance and the way he had of assuming that the world should fall in line with whatever he wanted. He was the boss who never made an effort to interact with those employees he felt were beneath him. He paid well not because he was a considerate and fair-minded guy who believed in rewarding hard work, but because he knew that money bought loyalty, and a loyal employee was more likely to do exactly what he demanded without asking questions. Pay an employee enough, and they lost the right to vote.

She hoped that he'd been telling the truth when he'd said that there would be no interaction between them because she couldn't think that they would have anything to talk about.

Then Katy thought about seeing him away from the confines of office walls. Something inside trembled and she had that whooshing feeling again, as if she had been sitting quietly on a chair, only to find that the chair was attached to a rollercoaster and the switch had suddenly been turned on. Her tummy flipped over; she didn't get it, because she really and truly didn't like the guy.

She surfaced from her thoughts to find that they had left the main roads behind and were pulling into a huge parking lot where a long, covered building opened onto an air field.

'I give you Lucas's transport...' Vicky murmured. 'If you look to the right, you'll see his private jet. It's the black one. But today you'll be taking the helicopter.'

Jet? Helicopter?

Katy did a double-take. Her eyes swivelled from private jet to helicopter and, sure enough, there he was, leaning indolently against a black and silver helicopter, dark shades shielding his eyes from the early-afternoon glare.

Her mouth ran dry. He was watching her from behind those shades. Her breathing picked up and her heart began to beat fast as she wondered what the heck she had got herself into, and all because she had stumbled across information she didn't even care about.

She didn't have time to dwell on the quicksand gathering at her feet, however, because with the sort of efficiency that spoke of experience the driver was pulling the car to a stop and she was being offloaded, the driver hurrying towards the helicopter with her bag just as the rotary blades of the aircraft began to *whop, whop, whop* in preparation for taking off, sending a whirlwind of flying dust beneath it.

Lucas had vanished into the helicopter.

Katy wished that she could vanish to the other side of the world.

She was harried, panic-stricken and grubby, because she hadn't had a chance to shower, and her jeans and shirt were sticking to her like glue. When she'd spoken to her mother on the phone, under the eagle eye of Vicky, she had waffled on with some lame excuse about being whipped off to a country house to do an important job, where the reception might be a bit dodgy, so they weren't to worry if contact was sporadic. She had made it sound like an exciting adventure because her parents were prone to worrying about her.

She hadn't thought that she really *would* end up being whipped off to anywhere.

She had envisaged a laborious drive to a poky holding pen in the middle of nowhere, with Internet access cruelly denied her. She hadn't believed him when he had told her to the contrary, and she certainly had not been able to get her head around any concept of an unplanned holiday unless you could call *incarceration* a holiday.

She was floored by what seemed to be a far bigger than average helicopter, but she was still scowling as she battled against the downdraft from the blades to climb aboard.

Lucas had to shout to be heard. As the small craft spun up, up and away, he called out, 'Small bag, Miss Brennan. Where have you stashed the books, the sketch pads and the tin of paints?'

Katy gritted her pearly teeth together but didn't say anything, and he laughed, eyebrows raised.

'Or did you decide to go down the route of being a good little martyr while being held in captivity against your will? No books…no sketch pads…no tin of paints…and just the slightest temptation to stage a hunger strike to prove a point?'

Clenched fists joined gritted teeth and she

glared at him, but he had already looked away and was flicking through the papers on his lap. He only glanced up when, leaning forward and voice raised to be heard above the din, she said, 'Where are you taking me?'

Aggravatingly seeming to read her mind, privy to every dark leap of imagination that had whirled through her head in a series of colourful images, Lucas replied, 'I'm sure that you've already conjured up dire destinations. So, instead of telling you, I'll leave you to carry on with your fictitious scenarios because I suspect that where you subsequently end up can only be better than what you've wasted your time imagining. But to set your mind at rest...'

He patted the pocket of the linen jacket which was dumped on the seat next to him. 'Your mobile phone is safe and sound right there. As soon as we land, you can tell me your password so that I can check every so often: make sure there are no urgent messages from the parents you're in the habit of calling on a daily basis...'

'Or from a married ex-boyfriend?' She couldn't resist prodding the sleeping tiger and he gave her a long, cool look from under the dark fringe of his lashes.

'Or from a married ex-boyfriend,' he drawled. 'Always pays to be careful, in my opinion. Now why don't you let me work and why don't you… enjoy the ride?'

CHAPTER THREE

THE RIDE PROBABLY TOOK HOURS, and felt even longer, with Katy doing her best to pretend that Lucas wasn't sitting within touching distance. When the helicopter began descending, swinging in a loop as it got lower, all she could see was the broad expanse of blue ocean.

Panicked and bewildered, she gazed at Lucas, who hadn't looked up from his papers and, when eventually he did, he certainly didn't glance in her direction.

After a brief hovering, the helicopter delicately landed and then she could see what she had earlier missed.

This wasn't a shabby holding pen.

Lucas was unclicking himself from his seat belt and then he patiently waited for her to do the same. This was all in a day's work for him. He turned to talk to the pilot, a low, clipped, polite exchange of words, then he stood back to allow her through the door and onto the super-yacht on which the helicopter had landed.

It was much, much warmer here and the dying rays of the sun revealed that the yacht was anchored at some distance from land. No intrusive boats huddled anywhere near it. She was standing on a yacht that was almost big enough to be classified as a small liner—sleek, sharp and so impressive that every single left wing thought about money not mattering was temporarily wiped away under a tidal wave of shameless awe.

The dark bank of land rose in the distance, revealing just some pinpricks of light peeping out between the trees and dense foliage that climbed up the side of the island's incline.

She found herself following Lucas as behind them the helicopter swung away and the deafening roar of the rotary blades faded into an ever-diminishing wasp-like whine. And then she couldn't hear it at all because they had left the helipad on the upper deck of the yacht and were moving inside.

'How does it feel to be a prisoner held against your will in a shabby cell?' Lucas drawled, not looking at her at all but heading straight through a vast expanse of polished wood and expensive cream leather furniture. A short, plump lady was hurrying to meet them, her face wreathed in smiles, and they spoke in rapid Italian.

Katy was dimly aware of being introduced to the woman, who was Signora Maria, the resident chef when on board.

Frankly, all she could take in was the breath-taking, obscene splendour of her surroundings. She was on board a billionaire's toy and, in a way, it made her feel more nervous and jumpy than if she had been dumped in that holding pen she had created in her fevered, over-imaginative head.

She'd known the guy was rich but when you were as rich as this, rich enough to own a yacht of this calibre, then you could do whatever you wanted.

When he'd threatened her with legal proceedings, it hadn't been an empty threat.

Katy decided that she wasn't going to let herself be cowed by this display. She wasn't guilty of anything and she wasn't going to be treated like a criminal because Lucas Cipriani was suspicious by nature.

She had always been encouraged by her parents to speak her mind and she wasn't going to be turned into a rag doll because she was overwhelmed by her surroundings.

'Maria will show you to your suite.' He turned to her, his dark eyes roving up and down her body without expression. 'In it you will find everything you need, including an *en suite* bathroom. You'll be pleased to hear that there is no lock on the outside of your room, so you're free to come and go at will.'

'There's no need to be sarcastic,' Katy told him, mouth set in a sullen line. Her eyes flicked to him and skittered away just as fast before they could dwell for too long on the dark, dramatic beauty of his lean face because, once there, it was stupidly hard to tear her gaze away.

'Correction—there's *every* need to be sarcastic after you've bandied around terms such as *kidnapped*. I told you that you should look on the bright side and see this as a fully paid two-week vacation.' He dismissed Maria with a brief nod, because this looked as though it was shaping up to be another one of *those* conversations, then he shoved his hands in his pockets and stared down at her. She looked irritatingly unrepentant. 'In the absence of your books, you'll find that there is a private home cinema space with a comprehensive selection of movies. There are also two swimming pools—one indoor, one on the upper deck. And of course a library, should you decide that reading is a worthwhile option in the absence of your computer.'

'You're not very nice, are you?'

'Nice people finish last so, yes, that's an accolade I've been more than happy to pass up, which is something you'd do well to remember.'

Katy's eyes narrowed at the bitterness in his voice. Was he speaking from experience? What experience? She didn't want to be curious about him, but she suddenly was. Just for a moment, she realised that underneath the ruthless, cool veneer there would be all sorts of reasons for him being the man he was.

'Nice people don't always finish last,' she murmured sincerely.

'Oh, but they do.' Lucas's voice was cool and he was staring at her, his head at an angle, as if examining something weird he wasn't quite sure about. 'They get wrapped up in pointless sentimentality and emotion and open themselves up to getting exploited, so please don't think I'll be falling victim to that trait while we're out here.'

'Get exploited?' Katy found that she was holding her breath as she waited for his answer.

'Is that the sound of a woman trying to find out what makes me tick?' Lucas raised his eyebrows with wry amusement and began walking. 'Many have tried and failed in that venture, so I shouldn't bother if I were you.'

'It's very arrogant of you to assume that I want to find out about you,' Katy huffed. 'But, as you've reminded me, we're going to be stuck here together for the next two weeks. I was just trying to have a conversation.'

'Like I said, I don't intend to be around much. When we do converse, we can keep it light.'

'I'm sorry.' She sighed, reaching to loop her long hair over one shoulder. 'Believe it or not, I can almost understand why you dragged me out here.'

'Well, at least *drag* is an improvement on *kidnap*,' Lucas conceded.

'I'm hot, tired and sticky, and sitting quietly at my desk working on my computer feels like a lifetime ago. I'm not in the best of moods.'

'I can't picture you sitting quietly anywhere.

Maybe I've been remiss in not getting out and seeing what my employees are doing. What do you think? Should I have left my ivory tower and had a look at which of my employees were sitting and meekly doing their jobs and which ones were pushing the envelope?'

Katy reddened. His voice was suddenly lazy and teasing and her pulses quickened in response. How could he be so ruthless and arrogant one minute and then, in a heartbeat, make the blood rush to her head because of the way he was able to laugh at himself unexpectedly?

She didn't know whether it was because she had been yanked out of her comfort zone, but he was turning her off and on like a tap, and it unsettled her.

After Duncan, she had got her act together; she had looked for the silver lining and realised that he had pointed her in the right direction of what to look for in a man: someone down-to-earth, good-natured, genuine. Someone *normal*. When she found that man, everything else would fall into place, and she was horrified that a guy like Lucas Cipriani could have the sort of effect on her that he did. It didn't make sense and she didn't like it.

'I think my opinion doesn't count one way

or another,' she said lightly. 'I can't speak for other people, but no one in my office actually expects you to swoop down and pay a visit.'

'You certainly know how to hit below the belt,' Lucas imparted drily. 'This your normal style when you're with a man?'

'You're not a man.'

Lucas laughed, a rich, throaty laugh that set her senses alight and had her pulses racing. 'Oh, no,' he murmured seriously. 'And here I was thinking that I was…'

'You know what I mean.' Rattled, Katy's gaze slid sideways and skittered away in confusion.

'Do I? Explain.' This wasn't the light conversation he had had in mind, but that wasn't to say that he wasn't enjoying himself, because he was. 'If I'm not a man, then what am I?'

'You're…you're my *captor*.'

Lucas grinned. 'That's a non-answer if ever there was one, but I'll let it go. Besides, I thought we'd got past the kidnap analogy.'

Katy didn't answer. He was being nice to her, teasing her. She knew that he still probably didn't trust her as far as he could throw her, but he was worldly wise and sophisticated, and knew the benefits of smoothing tensions and getting her onside. Constant sniping would bore him. He had been forced into a situation he hadn't banked on, just as she had, but he wasn't throwing temper tantrums. He wasn't interested in having meaningful conversations, because he wasn't interested in her and had no desire to find out anything about her, except what might impact on his business deal; but he would be civil now that he had told her in no uncertain terms what the lay of the land was. He had laughed about being called her captor, but he was, and he called the shots.

Instead of getting hot and bothered around him, she would have to step up to the plate and respond in kind.

They had reached the kitchen and she turned her attention away from him and looked around her. 'This is wonderful.' She ran her fingers over the counter. 'Where is Maria, your... chef?' She remained where she was, watching as he strolled to an over-sized fridge, one of two, and extracted a bottle of wine.

He poured them both a glass and nodded to one of the grey upholstered chairs tucked neatly under the metal kitchen table. Katy sat and sipped the wine very slowly, because she wasn't accustomed to drinking.

'Has her own quarters on the lower deck. I dismissed her rather than let her hang around listening to…a conversation she would have found puzzling. She might not have understood the meaning but she would have got the gist without too much trouble.'

Lucas sat opposite her. 'It is rare for me to be on this yacht with just one other person. It's generally used for client entertaining and occasionally for social gatherings. Under normal circumstances, there would be more than just one member of staff present, but there seemed little need to have an abundance of crew for two people. So, while we're here, Maria will clean and prepare meals.'

'Does she know why I'm here?'

'Why would she?' Lucas sounded genuinely surprised. 'It's none of her business. She's paid handsomely to do a job, no questions asked.'

'But wouldn't she be curious?' Katy couldn't help asking.

Lucas shrugged. 'Do I care?'

'*You* might not care,' she said tartly. 'But maybe *I* do. I don't want her thinking that I'm…I'm…'

'What?'

'I wouldn't want her thinking that I'm one

of your women you've brought here to have a bit of fun with.'

Lucas burst out laughing. When he'd sobered up, he stared at her coolly.

'Why does it matter to you what my chef thinks of you? You'll never lay eyes on her again once this two-week stint is over. Besides...' he sipped his wine and looked at her over the rim of his glass '... I often fly Maria over to my place in London and occasionally to New York. She has seen enough of my women over the years to know that you don't fit the mould.'

Katy stared at him, mortified and embarrassed, because somehow she had ended up giving him the impression that...*what*? That she thought he might fancy her? That she thought her precious virtue might be *compromised* by being alone with him on this yacht, when she was only here because of circumstances? The surroundings were luxurious but this wasn't a five-star hotel with the man of her dreams. This was a prison in all but name and he was her gaoler...and since when did gaolers fancy their captives?

'Don't fit the mould?' she heard herself parrot in a jerky voice, and Lucas appeared to give that some consideration before nodding.

'Maria has been with me for a very long time,' he said without a shade of discomfort. 'She's met many of my women over the years. I won't deny that you have a certain appeal, but you're not my type, and she's savvy enough to know that. Whatever she thinks, it won't be that you're here for any reasons other than work. Indeed, I have occasionally used this as a work space with colleagues when I've needed extreme privacy in my transactions, so I wouldn't be a bit surprised if she puts that spin on your presence here.' He tried and failed to think of the woman sitting opposite him in the capacity of *work colleague*.

You have a certain appeal. Katy's brain had clunked to a stop at that throwaway remark and was refusing to budge. Why did it make her feel so flustered; hadn't she, two seconds ago, resolved not to let him get to her? She wanted to be as composed and collected as he was but she was all over the place.

Why was that? Was it the unsettling circumstances that had thrown them together? Lucas was sexy and powerful, but he was still just a man, and male attention, in the wake of Duncan, left her cold. So why did half a sentence from a man who wasn't interested in her make her skin prickle and tingle?

She forced her brain to take a few steps forward and said faintly, 'I didn't realise men had a type.' Which wasn't what she had really wanted to say. What she had *really* wanted to say was *'what's your type?'*

Rich men were always in the tabloids with women dripping from their arms and clinging to them like limpets. Rich men led lives that were always under the microscope, because the public loved reading about the lifestyles of the rich and famous, but she couldn't recall ever having seen Lucas Cipriani in any scandal sheets.

'All men have a *type*,' Lucas informed her. He had a type and he was clever enough to know *why* he had that particular type. As far as he was concerned, knowledge in that particular area was power. He would never fall victim to the type of manipulative women that his father had. He would always be in control of his emotional destiny. He had never had this sort of conversation with a woman in his life before, but then again his association with women ran along two tracks and only two. Either there was a sexual connection or else they were work associates.

Katy was neither. Yes, she worked for him, but she was not his equal in any way, shape or form.

And there was certainly no sexual connection there.

On cue, he gazed away from her face to the small jut of her breasts and the slender fragility of her arms. She really was tiny. A strong wind would knock her off her feet. She was the sort of woman that men instinctively felt the need to protect.

It seemed as good a time as any to remember just the sort of women he went for and, he told himself, keeping in the practical vein, to tell *her,* because, work or no work, aside from his chef there were only the two of them on board his yacht and he didn't want her to start getting any ideas.

She was a nobody suddenly plunged into a world of extreme luxury. He'd had sufficient experience over the years with women whose brains became scrambled in the presence of wealth.

'Here's *my* type,' he murmured, refilling both their glasses and leaning towards her, noting the way she reflexively edged back, amused by it. 'I don't do clingy. I don't do gold-diggers, airheads or any women who think that they can simper and preen their way to my bank balance—but, more than that, I don't care for women who demand more than I am capable of giving them. I lead an extremely pressurised working life. When it comes to my private life, I like women to be soothing and compliant. I enjoy the company of high fliers, career women whose independence matches my own. They know the rules of my game and there are never any unpleasant misunderstandings.'

He thought of the last woman in his life, a raven-haired beauty who was a leading light in the field of international law. In the end their mutually busy schedules had put paid to anything more than a six-month dalliance although, in fairness, he hadn't wanted more. Even the most highly intelligent and ferociously independent woman had a sell-by date in his life.

Katy was trying to imagine these high-flying, saintly paragons who didn't demand and who were also soothing and compliant. 'What would constitute them demanding more than you're capable of giving them?' she asked impulsively and Lucas frowned.

'Come again?'

'You said that you didn't like women who demanded more than you were capable of giving them. Do you mean *love and commitment*?'

'Nicely put,' Lucas drawled. 'Those two things are off the agenda. An intellectually challenging relationship—with, of course, ample doses of fun—is what I look for and, fortunately, the women I go out with are happy with the arrangement.'

'How do you know?'

'How do I know what?'

'That they're happy. Maybe they really want more but they're too scared to say that because you tell them that you don't want a committed relationship.'

'Maybe. Who knows? We're getting into another one of those deep and meaningful conversations again.' He stood up and stretched, flexing muscles that rippled under his hand-tailored clothes. 'I've told you this,' he said, leaning down, hands planted squarely on the table, 'Because we're here and I wouldn't want any *wow* moments to go to your head.'

'I beg your pardon?'

'You're here because I need to keep an eye on you and make sure you don't do anything that could jeopardise a deal I've been working on for the past year and a half,' he said bluntly, although his voice wasn't unkind. He was unwillingly fascinated by the way her face could transmit what she was thinking, like a shining beacon advertising the lay of the land. 'I know you're out of your comfort zone but I wouldn't want you to get any ideas.'

Comprehension came in an angry rush... although, a little voice whispered treacherously in her head, *hadn't* she been looking at him? Had he spotted that and decided to nip any awkwardness in the bud by putting down 'no trespass' signs? She wasn't his type and he was gently but firmly telling her not to start thinking that she might be. 'You're right.' Katy sat back and folded her arms. 'I *am* out of my comfort zone and I *am* impressed. Who wouldn't be? But it takes more than a big boat with lots of fancy gadgets to suddenly turn its owner into someone I could *ever* be attracted to.'

'Is that a fact?'

'Yes, it is. I know my place and I'm perfectly happy there. You asked me why do I continue to work in a school? Because I enjoy giving back. I only work for your company, Mr Cipriani, because the pay enables me to afford my rent. If I could somehow be paid more as a teacher, then I would ditch your job in a heartbeat.' Katy thought that, at the rate she was going, she wouldn't have to ditch his job because *it* would be ditching *her*. 'You don't have to warn me off you and you don't have to be afraid that I'm going to start suddenly wanting to have a big boat like this of my own...'

'For goodness' sake, it's a *yacht*, not a *boat*.' And the guy who had overseen its unique construction and charged mightily for the privilege would be incandescent at her condescending referral to it as a boat. Although, Lucas thought, his lips twitching as he fought off a grin, it would certainly be worth seeing. The man, if memory served him right, had embodied all the worst traits of someone happy to suck up to the rich while stamping down hard on the poor.

Katy shrugged. 'You know what I mean. At any rate, Mr Cipriani, you don't want to be stuck here with me and I don't want to be stuck here with you either.'

'Lucas.'

'Sorry?'

'I think it's appropriate that we move onto first names. The name is Lucas.'

Flustered, Katy stared at him. 'I wouldn't feel right calling you by your first name,' she muttered, bright red. 'You're my boss.'

'I'll break the ice. Are you hungry, Katy? Maria will have prepared food and she will be unreasonably insulted if we don't eat what she has cooked. I'll call her up to serve us, after which she'll show you to your quarters.'

'Call her up?'

'The food won't magically appear on our plates.'

'I don't feel comfortable being waited on as though I'm royalty,' Katy told him honestly. 'If you direct me, I'm sure I can do whatever needs doing.'

'You're not the hired help, Katy.'

Katy shivered at the use of her name. It felt...*intimate*. She resolved to avoid calling him by his name unless absolutely necessary: perhaps if she fell overboard and was in the process of drowning. Even then she knew she would be tempted to stick to Mr Cipriani.

'That's not the point.' She stood up and looked at him, waiting to be directed, then she

realised that he genuinely had no idea in which
direction he should point her. She clicked her
tongue and began rustling through the drawers, being nosy in the fridge before finding
casserole dishes in the oven.

She could feel his dark, watchful eyes following her every movement, but she was relieved that he hadn't decided to fetch Maria,
because this was taking away some of her jit-
ters. Instead of sitting in front of him, perspiring with nerves and with nowhere to rest her
eyes except on *him,* which was the least rest-
ful place they could ever land, busying herself
like this at least occupied her, and it gave her
time to get her thoughts together and forgive
herself for behaving out of character.

It was understandable. Twenty-four hours
ago, she'd been doing her job and going
through all the usual daily routines. Suddenly
she'd been thrown blindfolded into the deep
end of a swimming pool and it was only natural for her to flounder before she found her
footing.

She could learn something from this because, after Duncan, being kind to herself
had come hard. She had blamed herself for
her misjudgements. How could she have gone

so wrong when she had spent a lifetime being so careful and knowing just what she wanted? She had spent months beating herself up for her mistake in not spotting the kind of man he had been. She had been raised by two loving parents who had instilled the right values in her, so how had she been sucked into a relationship with a man who had no values at all?

So here she was, acting out of character and going all hot and cold in the company of a man she had just met five seconds ago. It didn't mean anything and she wasn't going to beat herself up over it. There was nothing wrong with her. It was all a very natural reaction to unforeseen circumstances.

Watching her, Lucas thought that this was just the sort of domestic scene he had spent a lifetime avoiding. He also thought that, despite what he had said about his high-flying career women wanting no more than he was willing to give them, many of them had tentatively broached the subject of a relationship that would be more than simply a series of fun one-night stands. He had always shot those makings of uncomfortable conversations down in flames. But looking at the way Katy was pottering in this kitchen, making herself at home, he fancied that many an ex would have been thrilled to do the same.

'I like cooking,' she told him, bringing the food to the table and guilt-tripping him into giving her a hand because, as he had pointed out with spot-on accuracy, she *wasn't* the hired help. 'It's not just because it feels wrong to summon Maria here to do what I could easily do, but I honestly enjoy playing around with food. This smells wonderful. Is she a qualified chef?'

'She's an experienced one,' Lucas murmured.

'Tell me where we're anchored,' Katy encouraged. 'I noticed an island. How big is it? Do you have a house there?'

'The island is big enough for essentials and, although there is some tourism, it's very exclusive, which is the beauty of the place. And, yes, I have a villa there. In fact, I had planned on spending a little time there on my own, working flat-out on finalising my deal without interruptions, but plans changed.'

He didn't dwell on that. He talked, instead, about the island and then, as soon as he was finished eating, he stood up and took his plate to the sink. Katy followed his lead, noticing that his little foray into domesticity didn't last long, because he remained by the sink, leaning against it with his arms folded. She couldn't help but be amused. Just like the perplexed frown when he had first entered the kitchen, his obvious lack of interest in anything domestic was something that came across as ridiculously macho yet curiously endearing. If a man like Lucas Cipriani could ever be *endearing,* she thought drily.

'You can leave that,' was his contribution. 'Maria will take care of it in the morning.'

Katy paused and looked up at him with a half-smile. Looking down at her, he had an insane urge to...to *what?*

She had a mouth that was lush, soft and ripe for kissing. Full, pink lips that settled into a natural, sexy pout. He wondered whether they were the same colour as her nipples, and he inhaled sharply because bringing her here was one thing, but getting ideas into his head about what she might feel like was another.

'I'll show you to your cabin,' he said abruptly, heading off without waiting while she hurriedly stacked the plates into the sink before tripping along behind him.

Let this be a lesson in not overstepping the

mark, she thought firmly. They'd had some light conversation, as per his ground rules, but it would help to remember that they weren't pals and his tolerance levels when it came to polite chit chat would only go so far. Right now, he'd used up his day's quota, judging from the sprint in his step as he headed away from the kitchen.

'Have you brought swimsuits?' he threw over his shoulder.

'No.' She didn't even know what had happened to her bag.

Maria, as it turned out, had taken it and delivered it to the cabin she had been assigned. Lucas pushed open the door and Katy stood for a few seconds, looking at the luxurious bedroom suite, complete with a proper king-sized bed and a view of the blue ocean, visible through trendy oversized port holes. Lucas showed her a door that opened out onto a balcony and she followed him and stood outside in a setting that was impossibly romantic. Balmy air blew gently through her hair and, looking down, she saw dark waves slapping lazily against the side of the yacht. She was so conscious of him leaning against the railing next to her that she could scarcely breathe.

'In that case, there's an ample supply of laundered swimsuits and other items of clothing in the walk-in wardrobe in the cabin alongside yours. Feel free to help yourself.'

'Why would that be?'

'People forget things. Maria digs her heels in at throwing them out. I've stopped trying to convince her.' He raked his fingers through his hair and watched as she half-opened her mouth, and that intensely physical charge rushed through him again.

'Okay.'

'You have the freedom of my yacht. I'll work while I'm here and the time will fly past, just as long as we don't get in one another's way...'

CHAPTER FOUR

LUCAS LOOKED AT the document he had been editing for half an hour, only to realise that he had hardly moved past the first two lines.

At this point in time, and after three days of enforced isolation on his yacht, he should have been powering through the intense backlog of work he had brought with him. Instead, he had been wasting time thinking about the woman sharing his space on his yacht.

Frustrated, he stood up, strolled towards the window and stared out, frowning, at a panoramic view of open sea. Every shade of blue and turquoise combined, in the distance, into a dark-blue line where the sea met the skyline. At a little after three, it was still very hot and very still, with almost no breeze at all rippling the glassy surface of the water.

He'd looked at this very skyline a hundred times in the past, stared through this very window of his office on the lower deck, and had never been tempted to leave it for the paradise beckoning outside. He'd never been good at relaxing, and indeed had often found himself succumbing to it more through necessity than anything else. Sitting around in the sun doing nothing was a waste of valuable time, as far as he was concerned; and on the few occasions he had been on weekend breaks with a woman he had found himself enduring the time spent playing tourist with a certain amount of barely concealed impatience.

He was a workaholic and the joys of doing nothing held zero appeal for him.

Yet, he was finding it difficult to concentrate. If he had noticed Katy's delicate, ridiculous prettiness on day one, and thought he could studiously file it away as something he wasn't going to allow to distract him, then he'd made a big mistake because the effect she was having on him was increasing with every second spent in her company.

He'd done his best to limit the time they were together. He'd reminded himself that, were it not for an unfortunate series of events, the woman wouldn't even be on his yacht now, but for all his well-constructed, logical reasons for avoiding her his body remained stubbornly recalcitrant.

Perversely, the more uptight he felt in her company, the more relaxed she seemed to be in his.

Since when had the natural order of things been rearranged? For the first time in his life, he wasn't calling the shots, and *that* was what was responsible for his lack of focus.

Being stuck on the yacht with Katy had made him realise that the sassy, independent career women he dated had not been as challenging as he had always liked to think they were. They'd all been as subservient and eager to please as any vacuous airhead keen to burn a hole in his bank account. In contrast, Katy didn't seem to have a single filter when it came to telling him what she thought about…anything and everything.

So far, he had been regaled with her opinions on money, including his own. She had scoffed at the foolishness of racing towards power and status, without bothering to hide the fact that he was top of her list as a shining example of someone leading the race. She had quizzed him on what he did in his spare time, and demanded to know whether he ever did anything that was actually *ordinary*. She seemed to think that his lack of knowledge of the layout of his own private yacht's kitchen was a shocking crime against humanity, and had then opined that there was such a thing as more money than sense.

In short, she had managed to be as offensive as any human being was capable of being and, to his astonishment, he had done nothing to redress the balance by exerting the sort of authority that would have stalled her mid-sentence.

He had the power in his hands to ruin her career but the thought had not crossed his mind.

She might have been in his company for all the wrong reasons, but he was no longer suspicious of her motives, especially when she had no ability to contact anyone at all, and her openness was strangely engaging.

It was also an uncomfortable reminder as to how far he normally went when it came to getting exactly what he wanted, and that he had surrounded himself with people who had forgotten how to contradict him.

Without giving himself a chance to back out, he headed to his quarters and did the unthinkable: he swapped his khakis for a pair of swimming trunks that hadn't seen the light of day in months, if not years, and a tee-shirt.

Barefoot, grabbing a towel on the way, he headed up to the pool area where he knew Katy was going to be.

She had been oddly reticent about using the swimming pool and, chin tilted at the mutinous angle he was fast becoming accustomed to, she had finally confessed that she didn't like using stuff that didn't belong to her.

'Would you rather the swimsuits all sit unused in cupboards until it's time for the lot to be thrown away?'

'Would you throw away perfectly good clothes?'

'I would if it was cluttering up my space. You wouldn't have to borrow them if you'd thought ahead and brought a few of your own.'

'I had no idea I would be anywhere near a pool,' she had been quick to point out, and he had dealt her a slashing grin, enjoying the way the colour had rushed into her cheeks.

'And now you are. Roll with the punches, would be my advice.'

His cabin was air-conditioned, and as he headed up towards the pool on the upper deck he was assailed by heat. It occurred to him that she might not be there, that she might have gone against her original plan of reading in the afternoon and working on ideas for an app to help the kids in her class with their homework, something he had discovered after some probing. If she wasn't there, he'd be bloody disappointed, and that nearly stopped him in his tracks because disappointment wasn't something he associated with the opposite sex.

He enjoyed the company of women. He wasn't promiscuous but the truth was that no woman had ever had the power to hold his attention for any sustained length of time, so he had always been the first to do the dispatching. By which point, he was always guiltily relieved to put the relationship behind him. In that scenario, disappointment wasn't something that had ever featured.

Katy, with her quirky ways and forthright manner, was yanking him along by some sort of invisible chain and he was uneasily aware that it was something he should really put a stop to.

Indeed, he paused, considering that option. It would take him less than a minute to make it back down to his office where he could resume work.

Except…would he be able to? Or would he sit at his desk allowing his mind idly to drift off to the taboo subject of his sexy captive?

Lucas had no idea what he hoped to gain by hitting the upper deck and joining her by the pool. So what if she was attractive? The world was full of attractive women and he knew, without a shred of vanity, that he could have pretty much any of them he wanted.

Playing with his reluctant prisoner wasn't on the cards. He'd warned her off getting any ideas into her head so there was no way he was going to try to get her into his bed now.

Just thinking about that, even as he was fast shoving it out of his head, conjured up a series of images that sent his pulses racing and fired up his libido as though reacting to a gun at the starting post.

He reached out one hand and supported himself heavily against the wall, allowing his breathing to settle. His common sense was fighting a losing battle with temptation, telling him to hot foot it back to the office and slam the metaphorical door on the siren lure of a woman who most definitely wasn't his sort.

He continued on, passing Maria in the kitchen preparing supper, and giving a brief nod before heading up. Then the sun was beating down on him as he took a few seconds to appreciate the sight of the woman reclining on a deck chair, eyes closed, arms hanging loosely over the sides of the chair, one leg bent at the knee, the other outstretched.

She had tied her long, vibrant hair into some kind of rough bun and a book lay open on the ground next to her.

Lucas walked softly towards her. He hadn't seen her like this, only just about decently clothed, and his breathing became sluggish as he took in the slender daintiness of her body: flat stomach, long, smooth legs, small breasts.

He cleared his throat and wondered whether he would be able to get his vocal cords to operate. 'Good job I decided to come up here...' He was inordinately thankful for the dark sunglasses that shielded his expression. 'You're going pink. Where's your sunblock? With your skin colouring, too much sun and you'll end up resembling a lobster—and your two-week prison sentence might well end up being longer than you'd bargained for. Sun burn can be a serious condition.'

'What are you *doing* here?' Katy jack-knifed into a sitting position and drew her knees up to her chest, hugging herself and glowering from a position of disadvantage as he towered over her, all six-foot-something of bronzed, rippling muscle.

Her eyes darted down to his legs and darted away again just as fast. Something about the dark, silky hair shadowing his calves and thighs brought her out in a sweat.

She licked her lips and steadied her racing pulse. She'd kept up a barrage of easy chatter for the past few days, had striven to project the careless, outspoken insouciance that she hoped would indicate to him that she wasn't affected by him, *not at all,* and she wasn't going to ruin the impression now.

He'd warned her not to go getting any ideas and that had been the trigger for her to stop gaping and allowing him to get under her skin. She was sure that the only reason he had issued that warning was because he had noticed her reaction to him and, from that moment onwards, she had striven to subdue any wayward reactions under a never-ending stream of small talk.

To start with, she'd aimed to keep the small talk *very* small, anything to break the silence as they had shared meals. In the evenings, before he left to return to the bowels of the yacht, they'd found themselves continuing to talk over coffee and wine.

Her aim had been harder to stick to than she'd thought because something about him fired her up. Whilst she managed to contain her body's natural impulse to be disobedient—by making sure she was physically as far away from him as possible without being too obvious—she'd been seduced into provoking him, enjoying the way he looked at her when she said something incendiary, head to one side, his dark eyes veiled and assessing.

It was a subtle form of intellectual arousal that kept her on a permanent high and it was as addictive as a drug.

In Lucas's presence, Duncan no longer existed.

In fact, thanks to Lucas's all-consuming and wholly irrational ability to rivet her attention, Katy had reluctantly become aware of just how affected she had been by Duncan's betrayal. Even when she had thought she'd moved on, he had still been there in the background, a troubling spectre that had moulded her relationships with the opposite sex.

'I own the yacht,' Lucas reminded her

lazily. He began stripping off the tee-shirt and tossed it onto a deckchair, which he pulled over with his foot so that it was right next to her. 'Do you think I should have asked your permission before I decided to come up here and use the pool?'

'No, of course not,' Katy replied, flustered. 'I just thought that you had your afternoon routine and you worked until seven in the evening...'

'Routines are made to be broken.' He settled down onto the deck chair and turned so that he was looking at her, still from behind the dark shades that gave him a distinct advantage. 'Haven't you been lecturing me daily on my evil workaholic ways?'

'I never said that they were *evil*.'

'But you were so persuasive in convincing me that I was destined for an early grave that I decided to follow your advice and take some time out.' He grinned and tilted his shades up to look at her. 'You're not reacting with the sort of smug satisfaction I might have expected.'

'I didn't think that you would actually listen to what I said,' Katy muttered, her whole body as rigid as a plank of wood.

She wanted to look away but her greedy eyes

kept skittering back to him. He was just so un-
believably perfect. More perfect than anything
she had conjured up in her fevered imaginings.
His chest was broad and muscular, with just
the right dusting of dark hair that made her
draw her breath in sharply, and the line of dark
hair running down from his belly button elec-
trified her senses like a live wire. How was it
possible for a man to be so sexy? So sinfully,
darkly and *dangerously* sexy?

Every inch of him eclipsed her painful memories of Duncan and she was shocked that
those memories had lingered for as long as
they had.

Watching him, her imagination took flight.
She thought of those long, clever fingers stroking her, touching her breasts, lingering to cir-
cle her nipples. She felt faint. Her nipples were
tight and pinched, and between her legs liquid
heat was pooling and dampening her bikini
bottoms.

She realised that she had been fantasising
about this man since they had stepped foot on
the yacht, but those fantasies had been vague
and hazy compared to the force of the graphic
images filling her head as she looked away
with a tight, determined expression.

It was his body, she thought. Seeing him like that, in nothing but a pair of black trunks, was like fodder for her already fevered imagination.

Under normal circumstances, she might have looked at him and appreciated him for the drop-dead, gorgeous guy that he was, but actually she wouldn't have turned that very natural appreciation into a full-on mental sexual striptease that had him parading naked in her head.

But these weren't normal circumstances and *that* was why her pragmatic, easy-going and level-headed approach to the opposite sex had suddenly deserted her.

'Tell me about the deal.' She launched weakly into the first topic of conversation that came into her head, and Lucas flung himself back into the deck chair and stared up at a faultlessly blue, cloudless sky.

He was usually more than happy to discuss work-related issues, except right now and right here that was the last thing he wanted to do. 'Persuade me that you give a damn about it.' He slanted a sideways look at her and then kept looking as delicate colour tinged her cheeks.

'Of course I do.' Katy cleared her throat. 'I'm here *because* of it, aren't I?'

'Are you enjoying yourself?' He folded his arms behind his head and stared at her. 'You're only here because of the deal but, now that you *are* here, are you having a good time?'

Katy opened her mouth to ask him what kind of question that was, because how on earth could she be having a good time when life as she knew it had been turned upside down? Except she blinked and thought that she *was* having a good time. 'I've never been anywhere like this before,' she told him. 'When I was a kid, holidays were a week in a freezing-cold British seaside town. Don't get me wrong, I adored my holidays, but this is…out of this world.'

She looked around her and breathed in the warm breeze, rich with the salty smell of the sea. 'It's a different kind of life having a father who's the local parish priest,' she confided honestly. 'On the one hand, it was brilliant, because I never lacked love and support from both my parents, especially as I was an only child. They wanted more but couldn't have them. My mum once told me that she had to restrain herself from lavishing gifts on me, but of course there was always a limit to what they could afford. And besides, as I've told you, they always made sure to tell me that money wasn't the be-all and end-all.' She looked at Lucas and smiled, somewhat surprised that she was telling him all this, not that any of it was a secret.

Never one to encourage confidences from women, Lucas was oddly touched by her confession because she was usually so outspoken in a tomboyish, challenging way.

'Hence your entrenched disregard for money,' he suggested drily. 'Tell me about the down sides of life in a vicarage. I'll be honest with you, you're the first daughter of a man of the cloth I've ever met.'

The image of the happy family stuck in his mind and, in a rare bout of introspection, he thought back to his own troubled youth after his mother had died. His father had had the love, but he had just not quite known how to deliver it and, caught up in his own grief and his never-ending quest to find a substitute for the loss of his wife, he had left a young Lucas to find his own way. The independence Lucas was now so proud of, the mastery over his own emotions and his talent for self-control, suddenly seemed a little tarnished at the edges, too hard-won to be of any real value.

He dismissed the worrying train of thought and encouraged her to keep talking. She had a very melodic voice and he enjoyed the sound of it as much as he enjoyed the animation that lit up her ravishingly pretty, heart-shaped face.

'Down sides... Well, now, let me have a think...!' She smiled and lay down on the deck chair so that they were now both side by side, faces upturned to the brilliant blue sky above. She glanced across at him, expecting to see amusement and polite interest, just a couple of people chatting about nothing in particular. Certainly nothing that would hold the interest of a man like Lucas Cipriani. But his dark, fathomless eyes were strangely serious as he caught her gaze and held it for a few seconds, and she shivered, mouth going dry, ensnared by the gravity of his expression.

'So?' Lucas murmured, closing his eyes and enjoying the warmth and the rarity of not doing anything.

'So...you end up always knowing that you have to set a good example because your parents are pillars of the community. I could never afford to be a rebel.'

Even when she had gone to university her background had followed her. She'd been able to have a good time, and stay out late and drink with the best of them, but she had never slept around or even come close to it. Maybe if she hadn't had so many morals drilled into her from an early age she would have just got sex out of the way and then would have been re- laxed when it came to finding relationships. Maybe she would have accepted that not all relationships were serious, that some were des- tined to fall by the wayside, but that didn't mean they weren't worthwhile.

It was a new way of thinking for Katy and she gave it some thought because she had al- ways assumed, post-Duncan, that she would hang on to her virginity, would have learned her lesson, would be better equipped to make the right judgement calls.

Thinking that she could deviate from that path gave her a little frisson of excitement.

'Not that I was ever tempted,' she hurriedly expanded. 'I had too much experience of see- ing where drugs and drink and casual sex could lead a person. My dad is very active in the community and does a lot outside the vil- lage for down-and-outs. A lot of them ended up where they did because of poor choices along the way.'

'I feel like I'm talking to someone from another planet.'

'Why?'

'Because your life is so vastly different from anything I've come across.'

Katy laughed. Lying side by side made it easier to talk to him. If they'd been sitting opposite one another at the table in the kitchen, with the yacht rocking softly as they ate, she wasn't sure she would have been able to open up like this. She could spar with him and provoke him until she could see him gritting his teeth in frustration—in fact, she got a kick out of that—but this was different.

She couldn't even remember having a conversation like this with Duncan, who had split his time talking about himself and flirting relentlessly with her.

'What do you come across?' she asked lightly, dropping her hands to either side of the deck chair and tracing little circles on the wooden decking.

'Tough career women who don't make a habit of getting too close to down-and-outs,' Lucas told her wryly. 'Unless, in the case of at least a couple of them who were top barristers, a crime had been committed and they happened to be confronted with one of those down-and-outs in a court of law.'

'I remember you telling me,' Katy murmured, 'About those tough career women who never wanted more than you were prepared to give them and were always soothing and agreeable.'

Lucas laughed. That had been when he'd been warning her off him, just in case she got ideas into her head. On cue, he inclined his head slightly and looked at her. She was staring up at the sky, eyes closed. Her long, dark lashes cast shadows on her cheeks and her mouth, in repose, was a full, pink pout. The sun had turned her a pale biscuit-gold colour and brought out shades of strawberry blonde amidst the deep russets and copper of her hair. Eyes drifting down, he followed the line of her shoulders and the swell of her breasts under the bikini, which he had not really been able to appreciate when she had been hugging her knees to herself, making sure that as little of her body was on show as humanly possible.

The bikini was black and modest by any modern standard but nothing could conceal the tempting swell of her pert, small breasts, the barely there cleavage, the jut of her hip bones and the silky smoothness of her thighs.

Lucas didn't bother to give in to consternation at the hot, pulsing swell of his arousal which, had she only opened her big green eyes and cast a sideways glance at him, she'd have noticed was distorting his swimming trunks.

He'd acknowledged her appeal from day one, from the very second she had walked into his office. No red-blooded male could have failed to. He'd also noted her belligerence and lack of filter when it came to speaking her mind, which was why he had decided to take on babysitting duties personally until his deal was safely in the bag. When you took into account that she had shimmered into his line of vision as a woman not averse to sleeping with married men, one who could not be trusted, it had seemed the obvious course of action.

But he knew, deep down, that even though he had dismissed any notion of going anywhere near Katy the prospect of being holed up with her for a fortnight had not exactly filled him with distaste.

He wondered whether he had even played with the forbidden thought of doing what his body wanted against the wishes of his brain. Or maybe he had been invigorated just by the novelty of having that mental tussle at all. In his well-ordered life, getting what he wanted had never posed a challenge, and internal debates about what he should or shouldn't do rarely featured, especially when it came to women.

He thought that if she had lived down to expectations and proved herself to be the sort of girl who had no morals, and really *might* have tried her luck with him, he would have had no trouble in eating, breathing and sleeping work. However, she hadn't, and the more his curiosity about her had been piqued the more he had been drawn to her like a wanderer hearing the call of a siren.

Which was so not him *at all* that he almost didn't know how to deal with it.

Except, his body was dealing with it in the time-honoured way, he thought, and then hard on the heels of that thought he wondered what she would do if she looked and saw the kind of response she'd awakened in him.

Katy wasn't sure whether it was the sudden silence, or just something thick and electric in the air, but she opened her eyes and turned her head, her mouth already opening to say something bland and chirpy to dispel the sudden tension.

His eyes caught hers and she stopped breathing. She had a drowning sensation as she was swallowed up in the deep, dark, quiet depths of his eyes. Those eyes were telegraphing a message to her, or they seemed to be. Was she imagining it? She had no experience of a man like him. That cool, brooding, speculative expression seemed to be inviting a response, but was it? Flustered and confused, her eyes dipped...

And then there was no doubt exactly what message was being telegraphed.

For a few seconds, Katy froze while her mind went into free fall. He was *turned on*. Did he think that he could try it on and she would fall in line because she was easy? Who knew, he probably still believed that she was the sort who had affairs with married men, even though he surely should know better, because she had shared stuff with him, told him about her childhood and her parents and the morals they had instilled in her. Maybe he hadn't believed her. Maybe he had taken it all with a pinch of salt because he was suspicious and mistrustful.

She *wasn't* easy. And yet, unleashed desire flooded through her in an unwanted torrent, crashing through common sense and good intentions. *She wanted this man, this unsuitable man, and she wanted him with a craving that was as powerful as a depth charge.*

The shocking intensity of a physical response she had never, *ever* felt towards any man, including Duncan, scared the living daylights out of her. Mumbling something under her breath, she leapt to her feet, the glittering blue of the infinity pool beckoning like an oasis of safety away from the onslaught of confusion overwhelming her.

Heart hammering in her chest, she scrambled forward, missed the step that gave down to the smooth wood around the pool and found herself flying forward.

She landed with a painful thump, her knees stinging where she had grazed them after her airborne flight.

Clutching her leg, she watched in fascinated slow motion as Lucas strode towards her, every lean muscle of his body intent.

'What were you thinking?' he asked urgently, scooping her up and ignoring her protests that he put her down because she was *absolutely fine.* 'You took off like a bat out of hell. Something I said?'

He was striding away from the pool area, carrying her as easily as he would carry a couple of cushions. Katy clutched his broad shoulders, horribly aware that in this semi-folded position there were bits of her on view that made her want to die an early death from embarrassment.

One glance down and he would practically be able to see the shadow of one of her nipples.

'Where are you taking me?' she croaked. 'This is ridiculous. I tripped and fell!'

'You could have broken something.'

'I haven't broken *anything*!' Katy practically sobbed.

'How do you know?'

'Because if I had I wouldn't be able to walk!'

'You're not walking. I'm carrying you. How much do you weigh, by the way? You're as light as a feather. If I didn't see how much food you're capable of putting away, I'd be worried.'

'I've always been thin,' Katy said faintly, barely noticing where they were going because she was concentrating very hard on making sure no more of her bikini-clad body went on show. She felt she might be on the verge of passing out. 'Please just take me to my cabin. That would be fine. I can clean my knee up and I'll be as right as rain.'

'Nonsense. How could I live with myself if I didn't do the gentlemanly thing and make sure you're all right? I wasn't brought up to ignore damsels in distress.'

'I'm not one of those!'

'Here we are,' Lucas intoned with satisfaction. He kicked open the door and, when Katy tore her focus away from her excruciating attempts to keep her body safely tucked away in the swimsuit, she realised where he had taken her.

Away from the safety of the pool and straight into the hellfire of his private quarters.

CHAPTER FIVE

LUCAS'S CABIN WAS different from hers insofar as it was twice the size and unnervingly masculine: dark-grey silky throw on the bed, dark-grey pillows, built-in furniture in rich walnut that matched the wooden flooring. He laid her on the bed and she immediately wriggled into a sitting position, wishing that she had something to tug down to cover herself, but instead having to make do with arranging herself into the most modest position possible, back upright, legs rammed close together and hands primly folded on her lap.

Sick with tension, she watched him disappear into an adjoining bathroom, that made hers look like a shower cubicle, to return a minute later with a first-aid kit.

'This really isn't necessary...er... Lucas.'

'You managed the first name. Congratulations. I wondered whether you would.'

'I have a few grazes, that's all.'

He was kneeling in front of her and he began to feel her ankle with surprisingly gently fingers. 'Tell me if anything hurts.'

'Nothing,' Katy stated firmly. She gave a trial tug of her leg so that Lucas could get the hint that this was all pretty ridiculous and overblown but he wasn't having it.

Relax, she told herself sternly; *relax and it'll be over and done with in a second and you can bolt back to your cabin.* But how could she even begin to relax when those fingers were doing all sorts of things to her body?

The feathery delicacy of his touch was stirring her up, making her breathing quicken and sending tingling, delicious sensations racing through her body like little lightning sparks. She looked at his down-bent head, the raven-black hair, and had to stop herself from reaching out and touching it just to see what it felt like between her fingers.

Then she thought of the bulge of his arousal and felt faint all over again.

'I'm surprised you have a first-aid kit to hand,' she said breathlessly, tearing her fascinated gaze away from him and focusing hard on trying to normalise the situation with point-less conversation.

'Why?' Lucas glanced up briefly before con-tinuing with his exceedingly slow exploration of her foot.

'Because you don't seem to be the type to do this sort of thing,' Katy said honestly.

'It's essential to have a first-aid kit on board a sailing vessel. In fact, this is just one of many. There's a comprehensive supply of medical equipment in a store room on the mid-dle deck. You would be surprised at the sort of unexpected accidents that can happen when you're out at sea, and there's no ambulance available to make a five-minute dash to col-lect and take you to the nearest hospital.' He was working his way gently up her calf, which was smooth, slender and sprinkled with golden hair. Her skin was like satin and still warm from the sun.

'And you know how to deal with all those unexpected accidents?' Lucas's long, clever fingers were getting higher and, with each en-croaching inch, her body lit up like a Christ-mas tree just a tiny bit more. Any higher and she would go up in flames.

'You'd be surprised,' Lucas drawled. 'Your

knees are in a pretty terrible state, but after I've cleaned them up you should be fine. You'll be pleased to know that nothing's been broken.'

'I told you that,' Katy reminded him. 'Why would I be surprised?'

He was now gently swabbing her raw, torn skin and she winced as he patted the area with some oversized alcohol wipes, making sure to get rid of every last bit of dirt.

'Because,' Lucas said wryly, not looking at her, 'I get the feeling you've pigeonholed me as the sort of money-hungry, ambitious businessman who hasn't got time for anything other than getting richer and richer and richer, probably at the expense of everyone around him. Am I right?'

'I never said that,' Katy told him faintly.

'It's hard not to join the dots when your opening words to me were to accuse me of being capable of kidnapping you.'

'You *were* kidnapping me, in a manner of speaking!'

'Tell me how it feels to be a kidnap victim.' His voice was light and teasing as he continued to tend to her knee, now applying some kind of transparent ointment, before laboriously bandaging it and then turning his attention to foot number two. 'I always wanted to be a doctor,' he surprised her and himself by saying.

'What happened?' For the first time since she had been deposited on his bed, Katy felt herself begin to relax, the nervous tension temporarily driven away by a piercing curiosity. Lucas could be many things, as she had discovered over the past few days. He could be witty, amusing, arrogant and always, always wildly, extravagantly intelligent. But confiding? No.

'My father's various wives happened,' Lucas said drily. 'One after each other. They looked alike and they certainly were all cut from the same cloth. They had their eyes on the main prize and, when their tenure ran out, my father's fortune was vastly diminished. By the time I hit sixteen, I realised that, left to his own devices, he would end up with nothing to live on. It would have killed my father to have seen the empire his grandfather had built dwindle away in a series of lawsuits and maintenance payments to greedy ex-wives.

'I knew my father had planned on my inheriting the business and taking over, and I had always thought that I'd talk to him about that change of plan when the time was right; but, as it turned out, the time never became right because without me the company would have ended up subdivided amongst a string of gold-diggers and that would have been that.'

'So you gave up your hopes and dreams?'

'Don't get too heavy on the pity card.' Lucas laughed, sitting back on his heels to inspect his work, head tilted to one side. He looked at her and her mouth went dry as their eyes tangled. 'I enjoy my life.'

'But it's a far cry from being a doctor.' She had never imagined him having anything to do with the caring profession and something else was added to the swirling mix of complex responses she was stockpiling towards him. She thought that the medical profession had lost something pretty big when he had decided to pursue a career in finance because, knowing the determination and drive he brought to his chosen field of work, he surely would have brought tenfold to the field of medicine.

'So it is,' Lucas concurred. 'Hence the fact that I actually enjoy being hands-on when it comes to dealing with situations like this.'

'And have you had to deal with many of them?' She thought of him touching another woman, one of the skinny, leggy ones to whom those thong swimsuits forgotten on the yacht belonged, carefully stored just in case someone like her might come along and need to borrow one of them.

'No.' He stood up. 'Like I said, my time on this yacht is limited, and no one to date has obliged me by requiring mouth-to-mouth resuscitation whilst out to sea.' He disappeared back into the bathroom with the kit and, instead of taking the opportunity to stand up and prepare herself for a speedy exit, Katy remained on the bed, gently flexing both her legs and getting accustomed to the stiffness where the bandages had been applied expertly over her wounds.

'So I'm your first patient?'

Lucas remained by the door to the bathroom, lounging against the doorframe.

Katy was riveted at the sight. He was still wearing his bathing trunks although, without her even noticing when he had done it, he had slung on his tee-shirt. He was barefoot and he exuded a raw, animal sexiness that took her breath away.

'Cuts and grazes don't honestly count.' Lucas grinned and strolled towards her, holding her spellbound with his easy, graceful strides across the room. He moved to stand by the window which, as did hers, looked out on the blue of an ocean that was as placid as the deepest of lakes. His quarters were air-conditioned, as were hers, but you could almost feel the heat outside because the sun was so bright and the sky was so blue and cloudless.

'I'm sorry if I ruined your down time.'

'You never told me why you leapt off your deckchair and raced for the pool as though the hounds of hell were after you,' Lucas murmured.

She was in his bedroom and touching her had ignited a fire inside him, the same fire that had been burning steadily ever since they had been on his yacht. He knew why she had leapt off that deck chair. He had enough experience of the opposite sex to register when a woman wanted him, and it tickled him to think that she wasn't doing what every other woman would have done and flirting with him. Was that because she worked for him? Was that holding her back? Maybe she thought that he would sack her if she was too obvious. Or maybe she had paid attention to the speech he had given her at the start when he had told her not to get any crazy ideas about a relationship developing between them.

He almost wished that he hadn't bothered with that speech because it turned him on to imagine her making a pass at him.

Lucas enjoyed a couple of seconds wondering what it would feel like to have her begin to touch him, blushing and awkward, but then his innate pragmatism kicked in and he knew that she was probably playing hard to get, which was the oldest game in the world when it came to women. She had revealed all sorts of sides to her that he hadn't expected, but the reality was that she *had* had an affair with a married man. She'd denied that she'd known about the wife and kiddies, and maybe she hadn't. Certainly there was an honesty about her that he found quite charming but, even so, he wasn't going to be putting any money on her so-called innocence any time soon.

'It was very hot out there,' Katy muttered awkwardly, heating up as she recalled the pivotal moment when raging, uncontrolled desire had taken her over like a fast-moving virus and she had just *had to escape*. 'I just fancied a dip in the pool and unfortunately I didn't really look where I was going. I should head back to my room now. I think I'll give my legs a rest just while I have these bandages on—and, by the way, thank you very much for sorting it out. There was no need, but thanks anyway.'

'How long do you think we should carry on pretending that there's nothing happening between us?' Which, frankly, was a question Lucas had never had to address to any other women because other women had never needed persuading into his bed. Actually, it was a question he had not envisaged having to ask *her,* considering the circumstances that had brought them together. But he wanted her and there was no point having a mental tussle over the whys and wherefores or asking himself whether it made sense or not.

On this occasion, self-denial probably made sense, but Lucas knew himself and he knew that, given the option of going down the route of what made sense or the less sensible route of scratching an itch, then the less sensible route was going to win the day hands down every time.

He also knew that he wasn't a man who was into breaking down barriers and jumping obstacles in order to get any woman between the sheets—and why would he do that anyway?

This wasn't a game of courtship that was going anywhere. It was a case of two adults who fancied one another marooned on a yacht for a couple of weeks..

In receipt of this blunt question, presented to her without the benefit of any pretty packaging, Katy's eyes opened wide and her mouth fell open.

'I beg your pardon?'

'I've seen the way you look at me,' Lucas murmured, moving to sit on the bed right next to her, and depressing the mattress with his weight so that Katy had to shift to adjust her body and stop herself from sliding against him.

She should have bolted. His lazy, dark eyes on her were like lasers burning a hole right through the good, old-fashioned, grounded common sense that had dictated her behaviour all through her life—with the exception of those few disastrous months when she had fallen for Duncan.

The slow burning heat that had been coursing through her, the exciting tingle between her legs and the tender pinching of her sensitive nipples—all responses activated by being in his presence and feeling his cool fingers on her—were fast disappearing under a tidal wave of building anger.

'The way I *look at you*?'

'Don't be embarrassed. Believe me, it isn't usually my style to force anyone's hand, but we're here and there's a sexual chemistry between us. Are you going to dispute that? It's in the air like an invisible electric charge.' He laughed with some incredulity. 'You're not going to believe this, but it's something I can't remember feeling in a very long time, if ever.'

'And you think I should be *flattered*?'

Lucas frowned because this wasn't the reaction he had been expecting. 'Frankly, yes,' he told her with complete honesty.

Katy gaped, even though she knew very well why a woman would be flattered to be the object of attention from Lucas Cipriani. He was drop-dead gorgeous and a billionaire to boot. If he made a pass at a woman, then what woman was going to stalk off in the opposite direction and slam the door in his face? He probably had a queue of them waiting to be picked.

Her lips tightened because what he saw as a flattering, complimentary approach was, to her, downright insulting.

At least the creep Duncan had had the wit

to approach her a little less like a bull stampeding through a china shop.

But then, Katy concluded sourly, time wasn't on Lucas's side. They were here for a limited duration, so why waste any precious time trying to seduce her into bed the old-fashioned way?

'That's the most egotistical, arrogant thing I have ever heard *in my entire life*!'

'Because I've been honest?' But Lucas flushed darkly. 'I thought you were all in favour of the honest approach?'

'Who do you think I am?'

'I have no idea where you're going with this.'

'You think that you just have to snap your fingers and someone like me will dump all her principles and come running, don't you?'

'Someone like you?' But she had scored a direct hit, and he was guiltily aware that he *had* indeed compartmentalised her, however much he had seen evidence to the contrary.

'The sort of person,' Katy informed him with scathing distaste, 'Who needs a good, long lecture on making sure her little head doesn't get turned by being on a big, expensive boat—oh, sorry, *super-yacht*—with the great Lucas Cipriani! The sort of person,' she added for good measure, 'Who comes with a dubious reputation as someone who thinks it's okay to hop into bed with a married guy!' It made her even madder to think that she had fallen into the trap of forgetting who he really was, won over by his charm and the random confidences he had thrown her way which she had sucked up with lamentable enthusiasm.

And what made her even madder *still* was the fact that he had managed to read her so correctly! She thought she'd been the model of politeness, but he'd seen right through that and homed in laser-like on the fevered core of her that was attracted to him.

'You're over-analysing.' Lucas raked his fingers through his hair and sprang to his feet to pace the cabin before standing by the window to look at her.

'I am *not* over-analysing,' Katy told him fiercely. 'I know what you think of me.'

'You don't.' Unaccustomed to apologising for anything he said or did, Lucas now felt…like a cad. He couldn't credit how she had taken his interest in her and transformed it into an insult, yet he had to admit to himself that his approach had hardly been handled with finesse. He'd been clumsy, and in no one's wildest imagination could it have passed for *honesty*.

'I know exactly what you think of me! And you've got a damned cheek to imagine that I would be so easy that I'd just fall into bed with you because you happened to extend the invite.'

'I...I apologise,' Lucas said heavily, and that apology was so unexpected that Katy could only stare at him with her mouth open. He looked at her with a roughened sincerity and she fought against relenting.

Glaring, she stood up. Her good intentions of sweeping out of his cabin with her head held high, now that she had roundly given him a piece of her mind, were undermined by the fact that she was wearing next to nothing and had to hobble a bit because the grazes on her knees were killing her.

'Katy,' he murmured huskily, stopping her in her tracks. He reached out to stay her and the pressure on her arm where his fingers circled her skin was as powerful as a branding iron. She had to try not to flinch. Awareness shot through her, rooting her to the spot. 'I don't, actually, think that you're easy and I certainly don't take it for granted that you're going to fall into bed with me because that's the kind of person you are. And,' he continued with grudging sincerity, 'If there's a part of me that is still wary, it's because it's my nature to be suspicious. The bottom line is that I want you, and I might be wrong but I think it's mutual. So tell me…is it?'

He took half a step closer to her, looked down and suppressed a groan at the delicious sight of her delicate breasts encased in stretchy fabric. 'If I've misread the signals,' he told her, 'Then tell me now and I'll back off. You have my word. Nor will I let it affect whatever lies down the line in terms of your position in my company. Say no, and this is never mentioned again. It will never have happened.'

Katy hesitated. She so badly wanted to tell him that, no, she most certainly was *not* interested in him *that* way, but then she thought of him backing away and leaving her alone and she realised with a jolt how much she enjoyed spending time in his company when they were tossing ideas around and sparring with one another. She also now realised that underneath that sparring had been the very thread of sexual attraction which he had picked up with his highly developed antennae.

'That's not the point,' she dodged feebly.

'What do you mean?'

'I mean...' Katy muttered *sotto voce*, red-faced and uncomfortable, 'It doesn't matter whether we're attracted to one another or not. It would be mad for us to do anything about it. Not that I would,' she continued at speed, face as red as a beetroot. 'After Duncan, I swore to myself that I would never make the mistake of throwing myself into anything with some-one unless I really felt that they were perfect for me.'

'I've never heard such nonsense in my entire life,' Lucas said bluntly, and, feathers ruffled, Katy tensed and bristled.

'What's wrong with wanting the best?' she demanded, folding her arms, neither leaving the room nor returning to the bed, instead just standing in the middle as awkward as any-thing. He, on the other hand, looked totally at ease even though he was as scantily clad as she was. But then, he obviously wasn't the sort who gave a jot if his body was on display.

'Nothing's wrong with wanting the best,' Lucas concurred. 'But tell me, how do you intend to find it? Are you going to present each and every candidate with a questionnaire which they will be obliged to fill out before proceeding? I'm going to take a leap of faith here and assume that you didn't know about Powell's marital status. You went out with the man and presumably you believed that he was the right one for you.'

'I made a mistake,' Katy said defensively.

'And mistakes happen. Even if you're not being deliberately misled by a guy, you could both go out in good faith, thinking that it will go somewhere, only to discover that you hit obstacles along the way that make it impossible for you both to consider a life together.'

'And you're an expert because...?' Katy asked sarcastically.

'People are fond of self-deception,' Lucas delivered with all-knowing cool. 'I should know because I witnessed it first-hand with my father. You want something badly enough and you try and make it work and, if it all makes sense on paper, then you try all the harder to make it work. In a worst case scenario, you might actually walk up the aisle and then into a maternity ward, still kidding yourself that you've got the real deal, only to be forced to concede defeat, then cutting the ties is a thousand times more complicated.'

'You're so cynical…about *everything*.' She harked back to the lack of trust that had made him think that the only solution to saving his deal was to isolate her just in case.

'There's no such thing as the perfect man, Katy. With Powell, you got someone who deliberately set out to deceive you.' He shrugged. 'You might think I'm cynical but I'm also honest. I have never in my life set out to deceive anyone. I've never promised a bed of roses or a walk up the aisle.' He looked at her thoughtfully. 'You had a crap time with some guy who strung you along…'

'Which is why you should have believed me when I told you that I'd rather have walked on a bed of hot coals than have anything to do with him in my life again.'

'That's beside the point. At the time, I looked at the facts and evaluated them accordingly. What I'm trying to tell you is this: the world is full of men who will do whatever it takes to get a woman into bed, and that includes making promises they have no intention of keeping. With me, what you see is what you get. We're here, we're attracted to one another and that's all there is to it.'

'Sex for the sake of sex.' That was something she had never considered and surely *would* never consider. It contravened pretty much everything she had been taught to believe in. Didn't it? It was what Duncan had been after and that had repulsed her. Sex and love were entwined and to disentangle them was to reduce the value of both.

Lucas laughed at the disapproving, tight-lipped expression on her face. 'It could be worse,' he drawled. 'It could be sex for the sake of a happy-ever-after that is never going to be delivered.'

The air sizzled between them. Katy was mesmerised by the dark glitter in his eyes and could feel herself being seduced by opinions that were so far removed from her own. Yet he made them sound so plausible. Instead of giving her the freedom to enjoy a healthy and varied sex life, to take her time finding the right man for her, her experience with Duncan had propelled her ever further into a mind-set that rigidly refused to countenance anything but the guy who ticked all the boxes.

Wasn't Lucas right in many ways? How could you ever be sure of finding Mr Right unless you were prepared to bravely face down the probability that you might have to risk some Mr Wrongs first?

And who was to say that all Mr Wrongs were going to be creeps like Duncan? Some Mr Wrongs might actually be *fun*. Not marriage material, but *fun*.

Like Lucas Cipriani. He had Mr Wrong stamped all over him and yet...wouldn't he be fun?

For the first time in her life, Katy wondered when and how she had become so protective of her emotions and so incapable of enjoying herself in the way all other girls of her age would. Her parents had never laid down any hard and fast rules but she suspected now, looking back down the years, that she had picked things up in overheard conversations about some of the young women in distress they had helped. She had seen how unwanted pregnancies and careless emotional choices could destroy lives and she had consigned those lessons to the back of her mind, little knowing how much they would influence her later decisions.

Lucas could see the range of conflicting emotions shadowing her expression.

The man had really done a number on her, he thought, and along with that thought came another, which was that the first thing he would do, provided the deal went through, was to sling Powell out on his backside.

Whatever experiences she had had before the guy, he had clearly been the one she had set her sights on for a permanent relationship, and throwing herself into something only to find it was built on lies and deceit would have hit her hard.

For all her feisty, strong-willed, argumentative personality, she was a romantic at heart and that probably stemmed from her background. Sure she would have enjoyed herself as a girl, would have had the usual sexual experiences, but she would have kept her heart intact for the man she hoped to spend the rest of her life with, and it was unfortunate that that man happened to have been a married guy with a penchant for playing away.

'You may think that I don't have the sort of high moral code that you look for,' Lucas told her seriously. 'But I have my own code. It's based on honesty. I'm not in search of involvement and I don't pretend to be. You were hurt by Powell but you could never be hurt by me because emotions wouldn't enter the equation.'

Katy looked at him dubiously. She was surprised that she was even bothering to listen but a Pandora's box had been opened and all sorts of doubts and misgivings about that high moral code he had mentioned were flying around like angry, buzzing wasps.

'I'm not the type you would ever go for.' Lucas had never thought he'd see the day he actually uttered those words to a woman. 'And quite honestly, I second that, because I would be no good for you. This isn't a relationship where two people are exploring one another in the hope of taking things to the next level. This is about sex.'

'You're confusing me.'

'I'm taking you out of your comfort zone,' Lucas murmured, yearning to touch her, only just managing to keep his hands under lock and key. 'I'm giving you food for thought. That can't be a bad thing.'

Katy looked at him and collided with eyes the colour of the deepest, darkest night. Her heart did a series of somersaults inside her chest. He was temptation in a form she was finding irresistible. Every word he had said and every argument he had proffered combined to produce a battering ram that rendered her defenceless.

'You're just bored,' she ventured feebly, a last-ditch attempt to stave off the crashing ache to grab hold of what he was offering and hold on tight. 'Stuck here without a playmate.'

'How shallow do you think I am?' Lucas grinned, his expression lightening, his eyes rich with open amusement. 'Do you think I need to satisfy my raging libido every other hour or risk exploding? I'm tired of talking. I don't think I've ever spent this much time trying to persuade a woman into bed with me.'

'Should I be flattered?'

'Most definitely,' Lucas returned, without the slightest hesitation.

Then he reached out, trailed a long finger against her cheek and tucked some strands of coppery hair behind one ear. When he should have stopped and given her time to gather herself, because she was all over the place, he devastated her instead by feathering his touch along her collarbone then dipping it down to her cleavage.

Gaze welded to his darkly handsome face, Katy remained rooted to the spot. Her nipples were pinched buds straining against the bikini top. If she looked down she knew that she would see their roused imprint against the fabric. Her eyelids fluttered and then she breathed in sharply as he stepped closer to her and placed both of his big hands on her rib cage.

He had been backing her towards the bed without her even noticing and suddenly she tumbled back against the mattress and lay there, staring up at him.

She was about to break all her rules for a one-night stand and she wasn't going to waste any more time trying to tell herself not to.

CHAPTER SIX

EXCEPT KATY WASN'T entirely sure how she was going to initiate breaking all those rules. She'd never done so before and she was dealing with a man who had probably cut his teeth breaking rules. He'd made no bones about being experienced. Was he expecting a similar level of experience? Of course he was!

She quailed. Mouth dry, she stared at him in silence as he whipped off his shirt in one fluid movement and then stood there, a bronzed god, staring down at her. She greedily ate him up with her eyes, from his broad shoulders to his six-pack and the dark line of hair that disappeared under the low-slung swimming trunks.

Lucas hooked his fingers under the waistband of the trunks and Katy shot up onto her elbows, fired with a heady mixture of thrilling excitement and crippling apprehension.

What would he do if she were to tell him

that she was a virgin? *Run a mile*, was the first thought that sprang to mind. Katy didn't want him to run a mile. She wanted him near her and against her and inside her. It made her feel giddy just thinking about it.

In the spirit of trying to be someone who might actually know what to do in a situation like this, she reached behind her to fumble unsuccessfully with the almost non-existent spaghetti strings that kept the bikini top in position.

Lucas couldn't have been more turned on. He liked that shyness. It wasn't something with which he was familiar. He leant over her, caging her in.

'You smell of the sun,' he murmured. 'And I don't think I've ever wanted any woman as much as I want you right now.'

'I want you too,' Katy replied huskily. She tentatively traced the column of his neck then, emboldened, his firm jawline and then the bunched muscles of his shoulder blades. Her heart was thumping hard and every jerky breath she took threatened to turn into a groan.

He eased her lips apart and flicked his tongue inside her mouth, exploring and tasting her, and setting off a dizzying series of reactions that galvanised every part of her body into furious response. Her small hands tightened on his shoulders and she rubbed her thighs together, frantic to ease the tingling between them.

Lucas nudged her with his bulging erection, gently prising her legs apart and settling himself between them, then moving slowly as he continued to kiss her.

He tugged at her lower lip with his teeth, teasing her until she was holding her breath, closing her eyes and trembling like a leaf.

Katy didn't think that anything in the world could have tasted as good as his mouth on her and she pulled him against her with urgent hands.

She wished she'd rid herself of her bikini because now it was an encumbrance, separating their bodies.

She wriggled under him, reaching behind herself and, knowing what she wanted to do, Lucas obliged, urging her up so that he could tug free the ties. Then he rose up to straddle her and looked down, his dark eyes slumberous with desire.

Katy had never thought about sex without thinking about love and she had never thought about love without painting a tableau of the whole big deal, from marriage to babies in a thirty-second fast-forward film reel in her head.

Big mistake. In all those imaginings, her body had just been something all tied up with the bigger picture and not something needing fulfilment in its own right. The fact she had never been tempted had only consolidated in her head that sex was not at all what everyone shouted about.

Even the momentous decision that desire had propelled her into making, to ditch her hard and fast principles and sleep with him, had been made with no real prior knowledge of just how wonderfully liberating it would feel for her.

Yes, she had imagined it.

In practice, it was all oh, so wildly different. She felt joyously free and absolutely certain that what she was doing was the right thing for her to do.

Burning up, she watched Lucas as he looked at her. He was so big, so dangerously, *sinfully* handsome, and he was gazing at her as though she was something priceless. The open hunger in his eyes drove away all her inhibitions and she closed her eyes on a whimper as he leaned back down to trail his tongue against her collarbone.

Then he pinned her hands to her sides, turning her into a willing captive so that he could fasten his mouth on one nipple. He suckled, pulling it into his mouth while grazing the stiffened bud with his tongue.

This was sex as Katy had never imagined it. Wild, raw and basic, carrying her away on a tide of passion that was as forceful as a tsunami. This wasn't the physical connection from a kind, considerate and thoughtful guy who had wooed her with flowers and talked about a happy-ever-after future. This was the physical connection from a guy who had promised nothing but sex and would walk away from her the minute their stay on his yacht had come to an end.

His mouth and tongue against her nipple were sending piercing arrows of sensation through her body. She was on fire when he drew back to rid himself of his swimming trunks. The bulge she had felt pressing against her was impressively big, big enough for her to feel a moment of sheer panic, because how on earth could something so big fit inside her and actually feel good?

But that fear wasn't allowed to take root because desire was smothering it. He settled back on the bed and then tugged down the bikini bottoms.

Katy closed her eyes and heard him laugh softly.

'Don't you like what you see?' Lucas teased and she cautiously looked at him. 'Because I very much like what *I* see.'

'Do you?' Katy whispered, very much out of her depth and feverishly making all sorts of comparisons in her head between her boyish figure and the women he probably took to his bed. She wasn't going to dwell on it, but she wasn't an idiot. Lucas Cipriani could have any woman he wanted and, whilst she was confident enough about her looks, that confidence took a very understandable beating when she considered that the man in bed with her was every woman's dream guy. 'Sexy' didn't get more outrageous.

Lucas felt a spurt of pure rage against Powell, a man whose existence he had known nothing about a week ago. Not only had he destroyed Katy's faith in the opposite sex, but he had also pummelled her self-esteem. Any human being with functioning eyesight could have told her that she was a show-stopper.

He bent over to taste her pouting mouth whilst at the same time gently inserting his hand between her thighs.

She wasn't clean-shaven down there and he liked that; he enjoyed the feel of her soft, downy fluff against his fingers. He liked playing with it before inserting one long finger into her.

It was electrifying. He slid his finger lazily in long strokes, finding the core of her and the tight little bud that throbbed as he zeroed in on it. In the grip of sensations she had never known before, Katy whimpered and clutched him, all frantic need and craving. She was desperate to ride the crest of a building wave and her whimpers turned into soft, hitched moans as she began to arch her spine, pushing her slight breasts up, inviting him to tease a nipple with his tongue.

He released her briefly to fetch a condom from his wallet then he was over her, nudging her legs apart with his thigh and settling between them. Nerves firmly back in place, Katy smoothed exploratory hands along his back, tracing the hardness of muscle and sinew.

Her coppery hair was in tangles over her shoulders, spread like flames across the pillows. Lucas stroked some of the tangles back and kissed her.

'I want you,' Katy muttered into his mouth, and she felt him smile. Desire was a raging force inside her, ripping all control out of her grasp and stripping her of her ability to think straight, or even to think at all.

She felt his impatience and his need matching hers as he pushed into her, a deep, long thrust that made her cry out. He stilled and frowned.

'Don't stop,' she begged him, rising up so that he could sink deeper into her. She was so wet for him and so ready for this.

'You're so tight,' Lucas murmured huskily in a driven undertone. 'I can't describe the sensation, *mia bella.*'

'Don't talk!' Katy gasped, urging him on until he was thrusting hard, and the tight pain gave way to a soaring sense of pleasure as he carried her higher and higher until, at last, she came…and it was the most out-of-body experience she could ever have imagined. Wracked with shudders, she let herself fly until she weakly descended back down to planet Earth. Then, all she wanted to do was wrap her arms around him and hold him tightly against her.

Lucas was amused when she hugged him. He wasn't one for hugs, but there was something extraordinarily disingenuous about her and he found that appealing.

He gently moved off her and then looked down and frowned, his brain only slowly making connections that began to form into a complete picture, one that he could scarcely credit.

There wasn't much blood, just a few drops, enough for him to work out that none of that shyness and hesitancy had been put on. She'd blushed like a virgin because that was exactly what she was. He looked at her as the colour drained from her face.

'This is your first time, isn't it?'

For Katy, that was the equivalent of a bucket of cold water being poured over her. She hadn't thought that he would find out. She had vaguely assumed that if she didn't say anything then Lucas would never know that she had lost her virginity to him. She hadn't wanted him to know because she had sensed, with every pore of her being, that he wouldn't be thrilled.

For a man who didn't do commitment, and who gave warnings about the perils of involvement, a virgin would represent the last word in unacceptable.

She quailed and clenched her fists because making love to Lucas had been the most wonderful thing in her life, just the most beautiful, *right* thing she had ever done, and now it was going to be spoiled because, quite rightly, he was going to hit the roof.

She wriggled and tried to yank some of the covers up because there was no way she was going to have an argument with him in the nude.

'So what?' She eyed him mutinously under the thick fringe of her lashes and glowered. 'It's really no big deal.'

'No big deal?' Lucas parroted incredulously. 'Why didn't you tell me?'

'Because I know how you would have reacted,' Katy muttered, hugging her knees to her chest and refusing to meet his eyes for fear of the message she would read there.

'You know, do you?'

Katy sneaked a glance at him, and just as

fast her eyes skittered away. He was sprawled indolently on the bed, an in-your-face reminder of the intimacy they had just shared. She was covering up for all she was worth but he was carelessly oblivious to his nakedness.

'I wanted to do it.' She stuck her chin up and challenged him to argue with that. 'And I knew that if I told you that I'd never slept with anyone before you'd have run a mile. Wouldn't you?'

Lucas grimaced. 'I probably would have been a little cautious,' he conceded.

'Run a mile.'

'But I would have been flattered,' he admitted with even more honesty. 'I would also have been more gentle and taken my time.' He raked his fingers through his hair and vaulted out of the bed to pace the floor, before snatching a towel which was slung over the back of a chair and loosely settling it around his waist. Then he circled to sit on the bed next to her. 'It *is* a big deal,' he said gently. He took her hands in his and stroked her wrists until her clenched fists relaxed. 'And if I was a little rough for you, then I apologise.'

'Please don't apologise.' She smiled cautiously and stroked his face, and it was such an intimate gesture that she almost yanked her hand back, but he didn't seem to mind; indeed he caught her hand and turned it over so that he could place a very tender kiss on the underside of her wrist.

'You're beautiful, *cara*. I don't understand how it is that you've remained a virgin. Surely there must have been other men before Powell?'

Katy winced at the reminder of the man who had been responsible for landing them here together on this yacht. It was fair to say that, however hateful her memories of him were, they seemed a lot less hateful now. Maybe one day she might even mentally thank him because she couldn't see how she could ever regret having slept with Lucas.

'That was another of those down sides to having parents who were pillars of the community.' Katy let loose a laugh. 'There were always expectations. And especially in a tiny place, when you're growing up, everyone knows everyone else. Reputations are lost in the snap of a finger. I didn't really think about that, though,' she said thoughtfully. 'I just knew that I wanted the whole love and marriage thing, so my standards were maybe a bit on the high side.'

She sighed and smiled ruefully at Lucas, who was looking at her with such sizzling interest that every pulse in her body raced into overdrive.

'When Duncan came along, I'd just returned from university and I wasn't quite sure what direction my life was going to take. I remember my mother and I talking about the social scene at university, and my mum asking me about the boys, and something must have registered that I needed to take the next step, which was finding someone special.' She gazed at Lucas. 'I slept with you because I really wanted to. You said a lot of stuff...basically about seizing the day...'

'I had no idea I was addressing a girl who had no experience.'

'But, you see, that's not the point.' Katy was keen to impress this on him. 'The point is that you made me think about things differently. I know this isn't going anywhere but at least you were honest about that and you gave me a choice.' Duncan had denied her the truth about himself and, even if this was just a one night stand, which was something she had always promised herself she would never do, was it really worse to lose her virginity to Lucas than to a liar like Duncan?

She gazed up at him earnestly and Lucas lowered his head and very tenderly kissed her on the lips. He could have taken her again, right then, but she would be sore. Next time, he intended to make it up to her, to take his time. It blew his mind to think that she had come to him as a virgin. It was a precious gift and he knew that, even though he couldn't fully understand what had led her to give it to him.

'Yes, *cara,* there will be no "for ever after" with us but believe me when I tell you that, for the time we're together, I will take you to paradise and back. But before that…can I interest you in a shower?' He stood up and looked down at her slender perfection.

'With you?'

'Why not?' Lucas raised his eyebrows. 'You'd be surprised how different an experience it can be when you're in a shower with your lover.'

Katy shivered pleasurably at that word… *lover.* She shook her head and laughed. 'I think I'm going to relax here for a bit, then I'll go back to my cabin.'

Of course there would be no 'for ever

after'...and she was tempted to tell him that she understood that well enough without having to be reminded of it.

'Why?' Lucas frowned and then heard himself inviting her to stay with him, which was astonishing, because he had always relished his privacy, even when he was involved with someone. Sex was a great outlet, and his appetite for it was as healthy as the next man's, but when the sex was over his craving for his own space always took precedence over post-coital closeness. He'd never spent the night with a woman.

'Because I need to be on my own for a bit.'

Right then, Lucas felt that by the time they were ready to leave this yacht he would have introduced her to the joys of sharing showers and shown her how rewarding it could be to spend the night in his bed...

Katy had fallen into something of a sleep when she heard the bang on the door to her cabin. For the first time since she had arrived on Lucas's cruiser, she had retired to bed without anything to eat, but then it had been late by the time she had eventually left his cabin.

Having intended to sneak out while he was

showering, she had remained where she was
and they had spent the next few hours in one
another's arms. To his credit, he had not tried
to initiate sex again.

'I can show you a lot of other ways we can
satisfy one another,' he had murmured, and he
had proceeded to do just that.

In the end, *she* had been the one whose body
had demanded more than just the touch of his
mouth and the feel of his long, skilful fingers.
She had been the one to guide him into her and
to demand that he come inside her.

It had been a marathon session and she had
made her way back to her cabin exhaustedly,
still determined not to stay the night in his
room, because if she slept in her own bed then
she would somehow be able to keep control of
the situation.

'Katy! Open up!'

Katy jerked up with a start at the sound of
Lucas's voice bellowing at her through the
locked door. She leapt out of the bed, half-
drugged with sleep, and yanked open the door,
every fibre in her body responding with panic
to the urgency in his voice.

She looked at him in consternation. He was
in a pair of jeans and a black, figure-hugging

tee-shirt. Not the sort of clothes anyone would consider wearing for a good night's sleep. Her already panicked antennae went into overdrive.

'Lucas! What time is it?'

'You need to get dressed immediately. It's a little after five in the morning.'

'But why?'

'Don't ask questions, Katy. Just do it.' He forged into the room and began opening drawers, yanking out a pair of jeans, quickly followed by the first tee-shirt that came to hand. Even at that hour in the morning, it would be balmy outside. 'Maria is sick.' He looked at his watch. 'Very sick. It has all the makings of acute appendicitis. Any delay and peritonitis will kick in, so you need to dress and you need to dress fast. I can't leave you on this yacht alone.'

Katy dashed into the bathroom and began stripping off the oversized tee-shirt she slept in, replacing it with the jeans and tee-shirt she had grabbed from his outstretched hand.

'Do you think I might get up to no good if you're not around to keep an eye on me?' she asked breathlessly, only half-joking because that deeply intimate step she had taken with him had clearly not been a deeply intimate step for him. He was a man who could detach, as he had made perfectly clear.

'Not now, Katy.'

'How will we get her to the hospital?' She flushed, ashamed that her thoughts had not been one hundred percent on the woman of whom she had grown fond during the short time she had been on the yacht.

'Not by helicopter,' Lucas told her, his every movement invested with speed as he took her arm and began leading her hurriedly out of the bedroom. 'Too long to get my pilot here and nowhere to land near the hospital.'

They were walking quickly to a part of the yacht Katy hadn't known existed, somewhere in the bowels of the massive cruiser.

'Fortunately, I am equipped to deal with any emergency. And to answer your earlier question…' He briefly glanced down at her, rosy, tousled and so utterly adorable that she literally took his breath away. 'I'm not taking you with me because I think you might get up to no good in my absence. I'm taking you with me because if something happened to you and I wasn't around I would never forgive myself.'

Something flared inside her and she felt a lump in her throat, then she quickly told herself not to be an idiot, because that wasn't a declaration of caring; it was a simple statement of fact. If she was left alone on the yacht and she needed help of any sort, she would be unable to swim to shore and unable to contact him. How would he, or anyone in his position, be able to live with that?

Things were happening at the speed of light now. In a move she thought was as impressive as a master magician's sleight of hand, the side of the yacht opened up to reveal a speedboat, an expensive toy within an expensive toy. Maria, clearly in a great deal of pain but smiling bravely, was waiting for them and was soon ensconced, to be taken to the island.

Dawn was breaking as they hit the island, a rosy, blushing dawn that revealed lush trees and flowers and narrow, winding roads disappearing up sloping hills.

A car was waiting for them, a four-wheel drive with an elderly man behind the wheel. They reached the town in under half an hour and then Maria was met in Accident and Emergency and whizzed through in a wheelchair, everything moving as though orchestrated.

Katy had barely had time to draw breath. Only when the older woman had been wheeled into the operating theatre, and they were sitting in the small hospital café with a cup of coffee in front of them, did she begin to pay attention to her surroundings…and then it registered.

'Your name is all over this hospital…'

Lucas shifted uncomfortably and glanced around him. 'So it would seem.'

'But why?'

'My money went towards building most of it.' He shrugged, as though that was the most natural response in the world. 'My father's family owned a villa here and he spent his holidays on the island with my mother and me when I was very young. It's about the only thing my father didn't end up giving away to one of the ex-wives who fleeced him in their divorce proceedings. I expect he had strong sentimental attachments to it. There was a prolonged period when the villa got very little use but, as soon as I was able, I began the process of renovation. I have the money, so when the head of the hospital came to me for help it was only natural for me to offer it.'

It felt odd to be offering her this slither of personal information and for a few seconds he was uncomfortable with what felt like a loss of his prized self-control.

What was it about this woman that made him behave out of character? Not in ways that should be disconcerting, because she neither said nor did anything that raised red flags, but still...

He was intensely private, not given to sharing. However, this was the first time he had been on the island with any woman. He rarely came here but, when he did, he came on his own, relishing the feeling of being swept back to happier times. Was Katy's necessary presence here the reason why he was opening up? And why was he making a big deal of it anyway? he thought with prosaic irony. She couldn't help but have noticed his name on some of the wards, just as she couldn't have failed to notice how eager the staff were to please.

'The old hospital, which was frankly far from perfect, was largely destroyed some time ago in a storm. I made sure that it was rebuilt to the highest specification. The infrastructure here is not complex but it is essential it all works. The locals depend on exporting produce, and naturally on some tourism. The tourists, in particular, are the wealthy sort who expect things to run like clockwork. Including the hospital, should one of them decide to take ill.' He grinned. 'There's nothing more obnoxious than a rich tourist who finds himself inconvenienced.'

'And I'm guessing you don't include yourself in that category?' Katy teased. Their eyes met; butterflies fluttered in her tummy and her heart lurched. They hadn't had a chance to talk about what had happened because she had disappeared off to her own quarters, and here they were now, caught up in unexpected circumstances.

She had no idea whether this was something that would be more than a one-night stand. She hoped it was. She had connected with him and she would feel lost if the connection were abruptly to be cut. It panicked her to think like that but she had to be honest with herself and admit that Lucas was not the man she had originally thought he was. He still remained the last person on earth she could ever contemplate having an emotional relationship with, but he had shown her the power of a sexual relationship and, like a starving person suddenly led to a banquet, she didn't want the experience to end. Just yet.

But nothing had been said and she wasn't going to engineer round to the conversation.

'Do *you* think I'm obnoxious?' Lucas questioned softly and she blushed and squirmed, so very aware of those dark eyes fastened to her face.

'My opinion of you *has* changed,' Katy admitted, thinking back to the ice-cold man who had forced her hand for the sake of a deal. She thought that her opinion also *kept* changing. She didn't want to dwell on that, so instead she changed the subject. 'What about Maria? When will we find out what the outcome is?'

'There's every chance it will be a positive one.' Lucas glanced at his watch. 'I personally know the surgeon and there's no one better. I've contacted her family, who will be in the waiting area, and as soon as the operation is over I've asked to be called. I don't anticipate any problems at all. However...'

'However?'

'It does mean that there will be a small change of plan.'

'How do you mean?'

'We will no longer be based on the yacht. For a start, without Maria around, there will be no one to attend to the cooking and all the other little things she takes care of, and it's too late to find a replacement who can stay on board. So we'll have to relocate to my villa. I can get someone to come in on a daily basis and, furthermore, I will be on hand in case there are any complications following surgery.'

He paused. 'Maria worked for my father before he…began steadily going off the rails. My mother was very fond of her, so I've made sure to look out for her and her family, and also made sure to carry on employing her in some capacity when my father's various wives decided that they would rather have somewhat smarter people holding the fort in the various properties.'

His mobile phone buzzed and he held up one hand as he spoke in rapid Italian to the consultant, the concerned lines on his face quickly smoothing over in reaction to whatever was being said on the other end.

'All's gone according to plan,' he said. 'But, had she not reached the hospital when she did, then it would have been quite a different story. Now, why don't you wait here while I have a word with some of her family? I won't be long. I'll also arrange for your clothes and possessions to be transported to the villa.' He looked at her, head tilted to one side, then he patted his pocket. 'You can call your parents, if you like,' he said gruffly. 'I've been checking your phone, and I see that they've taken you at your word and not texted, but I expect they'd like to hear from you.'

He handed over the phone and her eyes shone, because more than anything else this demonstrated that he finally trusted her, and she found that that meant a great deal to her.

'What can I say to them?' she asked, riding high on the fact that she was no longer under suspicion. A barrier between them had been crossed and that felt good in the wake of what they had shared.

'Use your discretion,' Lucas told her drily. 'But it might be as well not to mention too many names, not that I think anything can go wrong with the deal at this stage. It's a hair's breadth away from being signed.' He stood up, leaving her with her mobile phone, and it felt like the greatest honour bestowed on her possible. 'I'll see you shortly and then we'll be on our way.'

CHAPTER SEVEN

LYING ON THE wooden deckchair by the side of the infinity pool that graced the lush grounds of his villa and overlooked the distant turquoise of the ocean, Lucas looked at Katy as she scythed through the water with the gracefulness of a fish.

The finalising of the deal had taken slightly longer than Lucas had anticipated, but he wasn't complaining. Indeed, he had encouraged his Chinese counterparts to take their time in sorting out all the essential details on which the takeover pivoted. In the meantime...

Katy swam to the side of the pool and gazed at him with a smile.

Up above, the sun had burnt through the early-morning clouds to leave a perfectly clear, milky, blue sky. Around them, the villa afforded absolute isolation. It was ringed with trees and perched atop a hill commanding views of the sea. Lucas had always valued his privacy and never more so than now, when he didn't want a single second of his time with her interrupted by so much as a passing trades-man. Not that any passing tradesman would be able to make it past the imposing wrought-iron gates that guarded the property.

He had dismissed all help, ensuring that the villa was stocked with sufficient food for their stay.

Just him…and her…

Right now, she was naked. He had half-ex-pected, after that tentative surrender four days ago when she had placed her small hand on his thigh and sent his blood pressure through the roof, that a three-steps-forward, one-step-back game might ensue. He had predicted a tussle with her virtuous conscience, with lust hold-ing the trump card, but in fact she had given herself to him without a trace of doubt or hesi-tation. He had admired her for that. Whatever inner battles she had fought, she had put them behind her and given generously.

'It's beautiful in here.' She grinned. 'Stop being so lazy and come and swim.'

'I hope that's not the sound of a challenge,' Lucas drawled, standing up, as naked as she was. He couldn't see her without his libido reacting like a lit rocket and now was no exception.

'Is sex *all* you ever think about, Lucas?' But she was laughing as she stepped out of the pool, the water streaming off her slick body.

'Are you complaining?' His eyes darkened and he balled his hands into fists. The urge to take her was so powerful it made him feel faint. He wanted to settle her on a towel on the ground and have her hard and fast, like a teenager in the grip of too much testosterone. Around her he lost his cool.

'Not at the moment,' Katy said breathlessly, walking straight into his arms. They had a lot of sex but, in fact, they also talked as well, and laughed, and enjoyed a level of compatibility she would never have thought possible when she had first met him.

He was still the most arrogant man she had ever met but there was so much more to him as well. She had no idea what was going to happen when they returned to London and she didn't think about it. Maybe they would carry on seeing one another…although how that would work out when she was his employee she couldn't quite fathom. The gossip would be out of control and he would loathe that.

For the first time in her life, Katy was living in the moment, and she wasn't going to let fear of what might or might not lie round the corner destroy her happiness.

Lucas cupped her pert bottom, which was wet from swimming, and kneaded it between his hands, driving her closer to him so that his rock-hard erection pushed against her belly.

She held him, played with him, felt the way his breathing changed and his body stiffened. She couldn't stop loving the way he reacted to her. It made her feel powerful and sexy and very, very feminine.

'I'm too big for deck-chair sex,' Lucas murmured.

'Who said anything about sex?' Katy breathed. 'We could just…you know…'

'I think I'm getting the picture.' He emitted a low, husky laugh and settled her on the cushioned deck chair, arranging her as carefully as an artist arranging a model he was about to paint, lying her in just the right place with her legs parted, hanging over either side of the chair, leaving her open for his attentive ministrations.

Then, sitting at the foot of the chair on his over-sized beach towel, he tugged her gently down towards his mouth and began tasting her. He slid his tongue into her, found the bud of her clitoris and licked it delicately, feathering little explosions of sensation through her, and he continued licking and teasing, knowing at which point she would begin to buck against his mouth as those little explosions became more and more impossible to control.

When he glanced up, he could see her small breasts, pointed and crowned with the dusky pink of her nipples, which were pinched from the water cooling on them. Her lips were parted, her nostrils flared as she breathed laboriously and her eyes were closed.

A thought flashed through his head. His condoms were nowhere to hand. What would happen if he were to sweep her up right now, hoist her onto him and let her ride them both to one of the body-shattering orgasms that they seemed strangely adept at giving one another? What if he were to feel himself in her without the barrier of a condom? Would it be such a bad thing? It wasn't as if pregnancy would be a certainty.

Shock at even thinking such a thing stilled

him for a second. He'd never had thoughts like that in his life before and it implied a lack of self-control he found disturbing.

He killed the wayward thought that had sprung from nowhere and drove a finger into her, rousing her deep inside, and feeling her begin to spasm as she began to soar towards a climax.

She came against his mouth, arching up with an abandoned cry of intense satisfaction, and then and only then did he allow her to touch him, with her mouth and with her hands.

The errant desire to take her without protection had been ruthlessly banished from his head but it left a lingering taste of unease in his mouth as they both subsided and flopped back into the pool to cool off.

Katy swam to Lucas but he stiffened and turned away, striking out into the water and rapidly swimming four lengths, barely surfacing for air as she watched from the side. He'd rejected her just then. Or maybe she'd been imagining it. Had she? He certainly hadn't done the usual and held her against him, coming down from a high with his body still pressed up against hers.

Sensitive to the fact that this was not a normal situation, that it was the equivalent of a one-night stand stretched out for slightly longer than the one night, Katy got out of the pool and walked over to her towel, anchoring it firmly around her so that she was covered up. Then she watched him as he continued swimming, his strong, brown body slicing through the water with speed and efficiency.

He didn't spare her a glance and after five minutes she retired to the villa and to the *en suite* bathroom which had been designated for her but rarely used, now she and Lucas were lovers.

The villa was magnificent, interestingly laid out with lots of nooks and crannies in which to relax, and huge, open windows through which breezes could circulate freely through the house. It lacked the slick sophistication of his yacht and was rather colonial in style with a stunning mixture of wood, billowing muslin at the windows, shutters and overhead fans. Katy loved it. She settled with her book into a rocking chair on the wide veranda that fronted the villa.

She kept waiting for Lucas to show up but eventually she gave up and nodded off. It was a little after four but still baking hot and, as always, cloudless.

Allowing her mind to drift, yanking it back every time it tried to break the leash and worry away at Lucas's reaction earlier on, she was scarcely aware of time going by, and it was only when she noticed the tell-tale signs of the sun beginning to dip that she realised that several hours must have passed.

In a panic, she scrambled to her feet and turned round, to find the object of her feverish imaginings standing framed in the doorway... and he wasn't smiling. Indeed, the humorous, sexy guy she had spent the past week with was noticeably absent.

'Lucas!' She plastered a smile on her face. 'How long have you been standing there? I was reading...er...I must have nodded off...'

Lucas saw the hurt beneath the bright smile and he knew that he had put it there. He had turned his back on her and swam off, and he had carried on swimming because he had needed to clear his head. When he'd finally stopped, she was gone and he had fought against the desire to seek her out because he was not going to allow a simple sexual liaison to get out of control. When they returned to

London, this would finish and his life would return to normal, which was exactly as it should be. So he'd kept his distance and that would have upset her. He clenched his jaw and focused on what really mattered now, which was a turn of events that neither of them could have predicted.

'You've been talking to your parents. What, exactly, have you told them?'

'Lucas, I have no idea what you're talking about.'

'Just try and think.' He moved to stand in front of her, the beautiful lines of his handsome face taut and forbidding. 'Did you tell either of them where you were? What you were doing here? Who you were with?'

'I…you're making me nervous, Lucas. Let me think…no; *no*. I just told Mum that I was in Italy and that it was lovely and warm and that I was fine and having a good time…'

'I have just spent the past hour on the phone with the Chinese company. It seems that they were told by Powell that I was the wrong kind of person to be doing business with—that I was the sort of guy who seduces innocent girls and shouldn't be trusted as far as I can be thrown. It would seem that news travelled and connections were made. Someone, some-where, figured out that we're here together and social media has taken the information right into Powell's hands and given the man am-munition to blow my deal sky-high at the last minute.'

The colour drained from Katy's face. When he said that 'connections were made', it was easy to see how. They had been into the lit-tle town several times over the past few days, checking on Maria and doing all sorts of tour-isty things. He could have been recognised and, whilst *she* wouldn't have been, someone could have sneakily taken a picture of them together and tagged them in something they posted online. The mind boggled.

'This is *not* my fault, Lucas. You know how pervasive social media is.' But it *was* her fault. She was the one with the connection to Dun-can and, if gossip had been spread, then who knew what her mum might have mentioned to anyone in the village? Someone might be friends with Duncan on Facebook or whatever. Guilt pinked her cheeks, but before she could go on the defensive he held up one imperious hand to close down her protest.

'I'm not going to waste time going back and

forth with this.' He frowned down at her and sighed. 'I'm not playing blame games here, Katy, and you're right: there's no privacy left anywhere. If anyone is to blame, then it's me, because I should have been more circumspect in my movements here. The place is small, I'm a well-known face, it's close to the busiest time of year for tourists and they have smart phones. But the fact remains that I have now been left with a considerable problem.

'No, perhaps I should amend that: when I say that *I* have a considerable problem, it might be fairer to say that we *both* have a considerable problem. Your ex approached Ken Huang and told him a story, and there's an underlying threat to go to the press and take public this sordid tale of a young, innocent girl being taken advantage of by an unscrupulous billionaire womaniser.'

Katy paled. 'Duncan wouldn't...'

But he would.

'He's played up your innocence to the hilt.'

'He knew...' Katy swallowed painfully. 'He knew that I was inexperienced. I never thought that he would use the information against me. I trusted him when I confided in him.'

In the midst of an unfolding nightmare,

Lucas discovered that the deal which should have been uppermost in his mind was over-shadowed by a gut-wrenching sympathy for her vulnerability, which Powell had thoroughly taken advantage of.

Lucas dragged over a chair to join hers and sat heavily, closing his eyes for a few seconds while he sifted through the possibilities for damage limitation. Then he looked at her.

'The man has an axe to grind,' Lucas stated flatly. 'Tell me why.'

'Does it matter?'

'In this instance, everything matters. If I need to use leverage, then I need to know where to apply it. I don't play dirty but I'm willing to make an exception in this case.'

'It ended really badly between me and Duncan.' She shot him a guilty, sidelong look before lowering her eyes. 'As you may have gathered. It wouldn't have been so bad if I'd found out about his wife and children *after* I'd slept with him, but I think he was doubly enraged that, not only did I find out that he was married, but he hadn't even succeeded in getting me into bed *before* I'd had a chance to find out.'

'Some men are bastards,' Lucas told her in

a matter-of-fact voice. 'It has to be said that some women leave a lot to be desired as well. It's life.'

'You mean those women your father married,' Katy murmured, distracted, thinking that on some level their approaches to life had been similarly tarnished by unfortunate experiences with the opposite sex. It was easy to think that, because you came from a wildly different background from someone, the things that affected the decisions you made had to be different, but that wasn't always the case. Money and privilege had been no more guarantee of a smooth ride in his case than a stable family background had been in hers.

Lucas shrugged. 'I have no more time for the gold-diggers,' he gritted. 'At least a guy with his head screwed on has a fighting chance of recognising them for what they are and can take the necessary precautions. You, I'm guessing, had no chance against a skilled predator. Continue.'

'I'd confided in my best friend,' Katy said, with a grimace. 'I felt such a fool. Claire was far more experienced than me, and she was livid when I told her about the messages I'd accidentally seen on his phone from his wife.

He'd made a mistake in leaving it on the table while he vanished off to the toilet when we'd been having a meal out. Up popped a reminder to phone the kids to say good night and to remember some party they were going to on the weekend. He'd told me he was going to be away on business. Weekends, he'd always said, were tricky for him because he was trying to kick-start a photography business and they were the only times he could do whatever he had to do—networking and the like—because he was at the bank during the week.'

'A skilled excuse,' Lucas said drily. 'The man obviously came with form.'

'That was what Claire said. She told me that I was probably not the first, which needless to say didn't make me feel at all better.'

It was as though she was looking at a very young, very naïve stranger from the advantageous position of someone who was much older and wiser. And she had Lucas to thank for that.

'Anyway, she started doing a little digging around. The world's a small place these days.' Katy grimaced. 'She found that he was a serial womaniser and she went to see his wife.'

'Ah.'

'I had no idea at the time that that was her plan, and afterwards she confessed that she didn't quite know what had prompted her to take such drastic action. But she was upset on my behalf and, in a weird way, upset on behalf of all the other girls he had conned into sleeping with him. His marriage fell apart on the back of that, so...'

'I'm getting the picture loud and clear. The ex who hates you and holds you responsible for the breakdown of his marriage now has the perfect vehicle for revenge put into his hands.'

'If I had told you the whole story in the first place, you would have realised that there was no chance I could have been any kind of mole. Then we wouldn't have ended up here and none of this would be happening now.'

Lucas smiled wryly. 'Really think that would have been how it would have worked?'

'No,' Katy answered honestly. 'You wouldn't have believed me. I would have been guilty until proven innocent.' At that point in time, he'd been a one-dimensional autocrat—ruthless, suspicious, arrogant. At this point in time...

She didn't know what he was and she didn't want to think too hard about it. They had a situation and she began to see all the nooks and crannies of it. If Duncan decided to take his revenge by publicising a tale of some sordid love tryst between Lucas and herself, not only would Lucas's deal be ruined but he would have to face the horror of the world gossiping about him behind his back. His reputation would be in tatters because, however much a lie could be disproved, mud inevitably stuck. He was the sort of guy who would claim to shrug off the opinions of other people, but that would be a heck of a lot to shrug off.

And it would all have been *her* fault.

Could she allow that to happen?

And then, aside from Lucas, there was the matter of her and her parents. They would never live it down. She felt sick thinking about their disappointment and the whispers that would circulate around the village like a raging forest fire blazing out of control. When she returned to see them, people would stare at her. Her parents would shy away from discussing it but she would see the sadness in their eyes.

She would be at the heart of a tabloid scandal: 'desperate virgin in sordid tryst with billionaire happy to use her for a few days before discarding her'. 'Sad and gullible innocent lured to a villa for sex, too stupid to appreci-ate her own idiocy'.

'Marry me!' she blurted out and then looked at him with wide-eyed dismay.

She jumped to her feet and began pacing the veranda, before curling onto the three-seater wicker sofa and drawing her knees up.

'Forget I said that.'

'Forget that I've received a marriage pro-posal?' Lucas drawled, strolling over to the sofa and sitting down, body angled towards her. 'It's the first I ever have...'

'It wasn't a marriage proposal,' Katy mut-tered, eyeing him with a glower, her cheeks tinged with heated colour.

'Sure about that? Because I distinctly heard the words "marry me".'

'It wasn't a *real* marriage proposal,' Katy clarified, hot all over. 'It just seemed that...if Duncan does what he's threatening to do—and I guess he will, if he's already started dropping hints to your client—then it's not just that your deal will be jeopardised—'

'Ruined,' Lucas elaborated for good mea-sure. 'Shot down in flames...dead in the water and beyond salvation...'

'All those things,' Katy mumbled, guilt

washing over her with tidal force. She breathed in deeply and looked him directly in the eyes. 'It's not even a marriage proposal,' she qualified. 'It's an *engagement* proposal. If we're engaged then Duncan can't spread any rumours about sordid trysts and he can't take your reputation away from you by implying that you're the sort of womaniser who's happy to take advantage of...of...an inexperienced young girl...'

He wasn't saying anything and she wished he would. In fact, she couldn't even read what he was thinking because his expression was so shuttered.

'Your deal can go ahead,' she plunged on. 'And you won't have to worry about people gossiping about you behind your back.'

'That sort of thing has never bothered me.'

Katy almost smiled, because that was just *such* a predictable response, then she thought about people gossiping about him and her heart clenched.

'What's in it for you?' Lucas asked softly.

'Firstly,' Katy told him with absolute honesty, 'You're here because of me, so this is pretty much my fault. Secondly, I know how much this deal means to you. Thirdly, it's not just about you. It's also about me. My parents would be devastated and I can't bear the thought of that. And *you* might not care about what other people think of you, but *I* care what other people think of me. I wouldn't be able to stay on at either of my jobs because of the shame, and I would find it really hard to face people at home who have known me all my life.'

It was slowly dawning on her that there had been something in his softly spoken words when he had asked her what would be in it for her, something she hadn't registered immediately but which she was registering fast enough now.

'It would work.' She tilted her chin at a defiant angle to rebut the hidden insinuation she had read behind his words. She might have been wrong in her interpretation but she didn't think so. 'And it would work brilliantly because there's no emotional bond between us. I mean, there's no danger that I would get it into my head that I was doing anything but role-playing. You could get your deal done, we could defuse a potential disaster and I would be able to live with myself.'

'You're presenting me with a business proposition, Katy?' He dealt her a slashing smile that threatened to knock her sideways. 'You, the ultimate romantic, are presenting me with a business proposition that involves a phoney engagement?'

'It makes sense,' she defended.

'So it does,' Lucas murmured. 'And tell me, how long is this phoney engagement supposed to last?' He couldn't help but be amused by this from the girl who typified everything that smacked of flowers, chocolates, soul mates and walks up the aisle in a frothy, meringue wedding dress. Then he sobered up as he was struck by another, less amusing thought.

Had he changed her into something she was never meant to be? He had shown Katy the marvels of sex without strings because it was something that worked for him, but had he, in the process, somehow *changed* her? For reasons he couldn't explain, he didn't like the thought of that, but he pushed those uneasy reservations to one side, choosing instead to go for the straightforward explanation she had given, which was that it was a solution that would work for her as well as it would work for him.

Katy shrugged. 'You still haven't said whether you think it's a good idea or not.'

'I couldn't have come up with something better myself.' Lucas grinned, then looked at her seriously. 'But you should know that I wouldn't ask you to do anything you feel uncomfortable about.'

Katy's heart did that weird, clenching thing again. 'I feel very comfortable about this and, as for how long it would last, I haven't given much thought to that side of things.'

'You'd be deceiving your parents,' Lucas pointed out bluntly.

'I realise that.' She sighed and fiddled with the ends of her long hair, frowning slightly. 'I never thought that the ends justified the means, and I hate the thought of deception, but, between the devil and the deep blue sea, this seems the less hurtful option.'

Lucas looked at her long and hard. 'So we're a loved-up couple,' he murmured, his dark eyes veiled. 'And in fact, so irresistibly in love with one another that we escaped for some heady time to my yacht where we could be together free from interruption from the outside world. Your colleagues at work might find it a little hard to swallow.'

'You'd be shocked at how many people believe in love at first sight.' Katy smiled. 'You know, just because *you're* such a miserable cynic when it comes to love, doesn't mean that the rest of us are as well...'

'So now I'm a miserable cynic,' Lucas drawled, reaching out to tug her towards him. 'Tell me how likely it is that you would fall head over heels for a miserable cynic?'

'Not likely at all!' Katy laughed, looking up at him, and her heart did that funny thing again, skipping a beat, which made her feel as though she'd been cruising along quite nicely only to hit a sudden patch of violent turbulence. 'I'm afraid what you have is a girl who could only fall head over heels for someone as romantic as she is!' She frowned and tried to visualise this special person but the only face to fill her head was Lucas's dark and devastatingly handsome one.

'If we're going to be engaged, then we need to get to know one another a whole lot better,' Lucas told her, still admiring the very practical streak which had led her to propose this very practical solution. Although, why should he be that surprised? She was a whizz at IT and that, surely, indicated a practical side to her that she herself was probably not even aware of.

He stood up, his fingers still linked with hers, and led her back through the villa and in the direction of his bedroom.

'What are you going to do with me once the engagement is over?' he murmured, toeing open his bedroom door, and then propelling her backwards to his bed while she tried to contain her laughter. 'I mean…' he lowered his head and kissed her, flicking his tongue into her mouth and igniting a series of fireworks inside her '… I'm assuming that, since you are the one with the clever plan to stage a fake engagement, you'll likewise be the one with the clever plan when it comes to wriggling out of it. So how will you dispose of me?'

He slid his hand under her tee-shirt and the warmth of her skin sent his body immediately into outer orbit. She wasn't wearing a bra, and he curved his big hand over her breast and gently teased her nipple until it was ripe and throbbing between his skilful fingers. They tumbled onto the bed, he settled her under him and straddled her so that he could see her face as he continued to tease her.

As usual, Katy's brain was losing the ability to fire on all cylinders, especially when he pushed up the tee-shirt and lowered himself to suckle her nipple. He looked up and caught her eyes, then flicked his tongue over the stiffened bud before devoting his attention to her pouting lips, kissing her again until she felt as though she was coming apart at the seams.

'Well?' He nuzzled the side of her neck and she wriggled and squirmed underneath him, hands on his waist, pushing into the waistband of his trousers and feeling his buttocks.

'Oh, I think we'll just drift apart,' Katy murmured. 'You know the sort of thing. You'll be working far too hard and you'll be spending most of your time in the Far East because of the deal you've managed to secure. I'll grow lonely and…who knows?…maybe I'll find some hunky guy to help me deal with my loneliness…'

'Not if I have any say in the matter,' Lucas growled, cupping her between her legs and rubbing until the pressure of his hand did all sorts of things through the barrier of her clothes.

'No,' Katy panted, bucking against his hand as she felt the stirrings of an orgasm building. 'I have to admit,' she gasped, her fingers digging into his shoulders, 'That finding another man wouldn't work, so perhaps you'll have to tire of me not being around and find someone else instead...'

And how she hated the thought of that although, she laughed shakily to herself, in the game of make-believe, what was the big deal? 'Let's not talk about this.' She tugged apart the button on his trousers and awkwardly tried to pull down the zipper. She looked at him and met his eyes. 'We can be engaged...for two months. Long enough to find out that we're not really compatible and short enough for no lasting damage.'

'You're the one calling the shots.' Lucas nipped her neck, reared up and yanked off his shirt, before proceeding to undress her very, very slowly and, when she was completely naked, pushing apart her thighs and gazing down for a few charged seconds at her stupendous nudity. 'And I like it... Now, stop talking. It's time for action, my wife-to-be...'

CHAPTER EIGHT

KATY HAD A week to think about what would happen when they arrived back in London. The surprise announcement of their engagement had hit the headlines with the fanfare of a royal proclamation. Sitting in the little square in the island's town, whilst they sipped coffees in the sunshine, she had scrolled through the newspapers on her phone and read out loud some of the more outrageous descriptions of the 'love at first sight' scenario which Lucas had vaguely hinted at when he had called, firstly, the anxious Ken Huang and then his personal assistant, who had been instructed to inform various elements of the press.

Lucas had been amused at her reaction to what, for him, was not entirely surprising, considering the extent of his wealth and eligibility.

Now, finally on the way back to London, with the helicopter that had delivered them to his super-yacht due to land in under half an hour, the events of the past few days no longer felt like a surreal dream that wasn't quite happening.

It was one thing to read the centre pages of the tabloids and marvel that she was actually reading about herself. It was quite another to be heading straight into the eye of the hurricane where, she had been warned by Lucas, there might still be some lingering press attention.

'At least there's been some time for the story to calm down a bit,' he had told her. 'Although there's nothing the public loves more than a good, old-fashioned tale of romance.'

'Except,' Katy had quipped, 'A good, old-fashioned tale of a break-up.'

Lucas had laughed but, now that the story was out in the open, now that her parents had been told and had doubtless told every single person in the village and beyond, Katy was beginning to visualise the fallout when the phoney engagement came to an end. In short, her theory about the end justifying the means was beginning to look a little frayed at the edges.

She had spoken to her parents every single day since the announcement and had played fast and loose with fairy stories about the way her heart had whooshed the minute she had clapped eyes on Lucas, the second she had *known* that it was the real thing. They had wanted details and she had given them details.

Katy knew that she would have to face all sorts of awkward questions when this charade was over. No doubt, she would be an object of pity. Her parents would be mortified that yet again she had been short-sighted enough to go for the wrong guy. If they ever happened to meet Lucas in the flesh, then they would probably suss that he was the wrong guy before the fairy tale even had time to come crashing down.

The world would feel sorry for her. Her friends would shake their heads and wonder if there was something wrong with her. And, inevitably, there would be malicious swipes at her stupidity in thinking that she could ever have thought that a relationship with someone like Lucas Cipriani could ever last the distance.

Who did she think she was?

And yet she was happy to close the door on reality because the thrill of living for the moment was so intense. It ate everything up. All her incipient doubts, and all her darkest imaginings about what lay beyond that two-month time line they had agreed upon, were swept aside and devoured by the intensity of appreciating every single second she had with him.

The timer had been set and every feeling, every sensation and every response was heightened to an excruciating pitch.

'I have something to tell you.' Lucas pulled her towards him. It still surprised him the way he couldn't get enough of her. 'Tonight we will be the main event at a black-tie ball.'

Katy stared at him in consternation. 'Tonight?'

'The Chinese company's throwing it. It seems that Ken Huang is keen to meet you, as are all the members of his family—and, in all events, with signatures now being put to paper, it's a fitting chance to celebrate our engagement publicly as well as the closing of the deal. Your parents, naturally have been invited to attend, as have your friends and other family members. Have you got any other family, as a matter of interest?'

Katy laughed. 'Shouldn't you know that?'

'I should,' Lucas said gravely, 'But these things sometimes get overlooked in a hectic whirlwind romance.' She was wearing a little blue top and some faded cut-off jeans and, if they had been anywhere remotely private, he would have enjoyed nothing better than getting her out of both items of clothing.

'I've never been to a ball in my life before,' Katy confided, brushing aside her unease because not only would she have to mix with people she had no experience of mixing with but she would also be *on show*. 'It would be nice if Mum and Dad came, but honestly, I doubt they will. It wouldn't be their thing at all, and my dad's calendar is so packed with community stuff that he will struggle to free up the time without more advance warning.' She sighed and looked at him a little worriedly.

Lucas was overwhelmed by a sudden surge of protectiveness that came from nowhere and left him winded. He drew back slightly, confused by an emotion that had no place within his vocabulary. 'It's no big deal.'

'It's no big deal *for you*,' Katy told him gently. 'It's a huge deal *for me*.'

Lucas frowned. 'I thought everyone liked that sort of thing,' he admitted. 'There'll be a host of well-known faces there.'

Katy laughed because his self-assurance was so deeply ingrained that it beggared belief. 'Part of me didn't really think about how this would play out when we returned to London,' she admitted. 'It felt very…unreal when we were in Italy.'

'Yes it did,' Lucas agreed. 'Yet surely you would have expected a certain amount of outside attention focused on us…?'

He knew that this very naivety was something he found intensely attractive about her. Having experienced all the trappings of extreme wealth for the past fortnight, she still hadn't joined the dots to work out what came as part and parcel of that extreme wealth, and intrusive media coverage at a time like this was one of those things. Not to mention a very necessary and unfortunately inevitable black-tie event. He decided that it would be unwise to mention just how much attention would be focused on her, and not just from reporters waiting outside the venue.

'You're going to tell me I'm an idiot.'

'I've discovered I quite like idiots.' He touched her thigh with his finger and Katy shivered and came close to forgetting all her apprehensions and doubts. They might be acting out a charade when it came to an emotional involvement with one another, or at least the sort of emotional involvement that came under the heading of 'love', but when it came to physical involvement there was no reporter who wouldn't be convinced that what they had was the real deal.

'When we get to the airfield, don't be surprised if there are one or two reporters waiting and just follow my lead. Don't say anything. I've given them enough fodder to be getting on with. They can take a couple of pictures and that'll have to do. In a week, we'll be yesterday's salacious gossip. And don't worry—you'll be fine. You never run yourself down, and you're the only woman I've ever met who gets a kick out of telling me exactly what she thinks of me. Don't be intimidated by the occasion.' He laughed and said, only partly in jest, 'If you're not intimidated by me, then you can handle anything.'

Buoyed up by Lucas's vote of confidence, Katy watched as the door of the helicopter was pushed open to blue sky, a cooler temperature than they had left behind and a fleet of reporters who flocked towards them like a pack of wolves scenting a fresh kill.

Katy automatically cringed back and felt his arm loop through hers, gently squeezing her reassuringly as he batted aside questions and guided her towards the black car waiting for them.

A reporter yelled out asking to see the engagement ring. Katy gazed in alarm at her ring-free finger and began stumbling out something vague when Lucas cut into her stammering non-answer, drawing briefly to a halt and smoothly explaining that the jeweller's was going to be their first stop as soon as they were back in the city.

'But it won't be, will it?' she asked as soon as they were settled into the back of the car with the glass partition firmly shut between the driver and them.

'Do you think you're going to be able to get away without a ring on your finger at the ball?' Lucas said wryly. 'Brace yourself for a lot more attention than you got from those reporters back there at the air field.' He settled against the door, inclining his big body towards her.

She was waking up to life in *his world*. Not the bubble they had shared in the villa, and even more so on his yacht, where they'd been secluded and tucked away from prying eyes, but the real world in which he moved. She was going to be thrown into the deep end and it couldn't be helped. Would she be able to swim or would she flounder?

He had told her that she would be fine and again he felt it—that strong streak of protectiveness when he thought about her lost and trying to find her way in a world that was probably alien to her. He knew from experience that the people who occupied his world could be harsh and critical. He disliked the thought of seeing her hurt, even though the practical side of him knew that the disingenuousness that he found so intensely appealing would be a possible weakness under the harsh glare of real life, away from the pleasant bubble in which they had been cocooned.

'We can stop for a bite to eat, get freshened up at my place and then head out to the jeweller's, or else we can go directly there. And, on the subject of things to be bought, there'll be a small matter of something for you to wear this evening.'

'Something to wear…'

'Fancy. Long.' He shrugged. 'Naturally you won't be expected to foot the bill for whatever you get, Katy.' He wondered whether he should go with her, hold her hand.

Katy stilled and wondered how the insertion of money into the conversation could make the hairs on the back of her neck stand on end. It felt as though something was shifting between them, although she couldn't quite put her finger on what that *something* was.

'Of course.' Politeness had crept into her voice where before there had only been teasing warmth, and she didn't like it. But how could she pretend that things hadn't changed between them? They had embarked on a course of action that wasn't *real* and perhaps that was shaping her reactions towards him, making her prickly and on edge.

Yes, she was free to touch, but there were now inbuilt constraints to their relationship. They were supposed to project a certain image, and that image would require her to step out of her comfort zone and do things she wasn't accustomed to doing. She was going to be on show and Lucas was right—she wasn't in the habit of running herself down and she wasn't going to start now. If she was hesitant and apprehensive, then that was understandable, but she wasn't going to let sudden insecurities dictate how she behaved.

'I think I'd rather get the ring and the outfit out of the way, then at least I can spend the afternoon relaxing, although I don't suppose I'll have much time to put my feet up.' She sighed and said with heartfelt honesty, 'I never thought I'd be getting an engagement ring under these circumstances.' She looked at her finger and tried to think back to those days when she had stupidly believed that Duncan was the man for her. Then she glanced across at Lucas and shivered. He was so ridiculously handsome, so madly self-assured. He oozed sex appeal and her body wasn't her own when she was around him. When she was around him, her body wanted to be his and only his.

What if this were a real engagement, not some crazy charade to appease other people?

She was suddenly filled with a deep, shattering yearning for a real relationship and for everything that came with it. This time it wasn't just for a relationship to rescue her from making decisions about her future, which had been the reason she'd allowed herself to be swept away by fantasies about tying the knot with Duncan.

Time slowed. It felt so right with Lucas and yet he was so wrong. How was that possible? She had proposed a course of action that had made sense, and she had imagined she could handle it with cool and aplomb because what she felt for Lucas was lust and lust was a passing fever. But looking at him now, feeling his living, breathing warmth next to her... The time they had spent together flickered like a slow-motion movie in her head: the laughter they had shared; the conversations they had had; their lazy love-making and the soaring happiness that had engulfed her when she had lain, warm and sated, in his arms.

Katy was overcome with *wanting more*. She transferred her gaze blindly down to her finger and pictured that ring on it, and then her imagination took flight and she thought of so much more. She imagined him on bended knee...smiling up at her...wanting her to be his wife *for real* and not a pretend fiancée for two months...

She loved him. She loved him and he certainly didn't love her. Sick panic filled her at the horror that she might have opened the door for hurt, and on a far bigger scale than Duncan had delivered. Indeed, next to Lucas, Duncan was a pale, ineffectual ghost and obviously one who had not taught her any lessons at all.

Lucas noted the emotions flickering across

her face and instantly barriers that had been
carefully crafted over many years fell back into
place. He didn't do emotion. Emotions made
you lose focus, sapped your strength, made
you vulnerable in ways that were destructive.
Gold-diggers had come close to destroying
his business, but it had been his father's own
emotions that had finally let him down. Lucas
could feel himself mentally stepping back and
he had the oddest feeling that just for a while
there he had been standing too close to an inferno, the existence of which he had been unaware.

He leaned forward, slid the glass partition
to one side and instructed the driver to deliver
them to a jeweller Katy had never heard of but
which, she guessed, would be the sort of place
to deal with very, very exclusive clients.

'Where are we?' she asked forty-five minutes later, during which time Lucas had worked
on his computer, catching up on transactions
he had largely ignored while they had been
in Italy, he'd told her without glancing at her.

'Jeweller's,' he said. 'Stop number one.'

'It doesn't look like a jeweller's...'

'We wealthy folk like to think that we don't
frequent the sort of obvious places every other

normal person does,' Lucas said, back in his comfort zone, back in control.

'Interesting story here,' he expanded as the car drew to a smooth halt and the driver stepped out to open the door for her. 'The woman who owns the place, Vanessa Bart, inherited it from her father and employed a young girl to work here—Abigail Christie. Long story but, to summarise, it turned out that she had a child from my friend Leandro, unbeknown to him, and like star-crossed lovers they ended up meeting again quite by chance, falling in love and getting married a while back.'

'The fairy tale,' Katy said wistfully as they were allowed into a shop that was as wonderful as Aladdin's cave. 'It's nice that it happens now and again.' She smiled and whispered, 'There's hope for me yet.'

'Wrong sentiment for a woman on the verge of wearing an engagement ring from the man of her dreams.' Lucas's voice was less amused than he would have liked. He laughed shortly and then they were being ushered into the wonderful den of exquisite gems and jewels, tray after tray of diamond rings being brought out for her to inspect, none of them bearing anything so trashy as a price tag.

Lucas watched her down-bent head as she looked at the offerings. He was a man on the verge of an engagement and, whether it was phoney or not, he suddenly had that dangerous, destabilising feeling again…the sensation of getting close to a raging inferno, an inferno he couldn't see and therefore could not protect himself against. He shifted uneasily and was relieved when she finally chose the smallest, yet as it turned out one of the dearest, of the rings.

'Rest assured,' Katy said quietly as they were once again passengers in the back seat of the car, 'That I won't be taking the ring with me when this is all over.'

'Let's just live a day at a time.' Lucas was still unsettled and frankly eager now to get to his office where he wouldn't be inconvenienced by feelings he couldn't explain. 'Before we start deciding who gets what when we're dividing the spoils.'

'Where do we go for the dress?'

'Selfridges. I've already got my PA to arrange a personal shopper for you.'

'A personal shopper…'

'I have to get to my office, so will be unable to accompany you.'

As their eyes tangled, Katy felt the thrill of being here next to him, even if that thrill was underlain with the presence of danger and the prospect of unhappiness ahead. 'I wouldn't expect you to come with me. I don't need you to hold my hand. If you let me have the name of the person I'm supposed to meet, then I can take it from there. And, after I've done all the other stuff I'm supposed to do, then I think I'm going to head back to my place and get changed there.'

Begin stepping away, she thought sadly. *Begin a process of detachment. Protect yourself.*

Lucas was already putting the romance of Italy behind him. There would be a ring on her finger, but he wasn't going to be hankering for all that undiluted time in each other's company they had had at his villa. He was slipping back to his reality and that involved distancing himself from her; Katy could sense that.

'Why?' Lucas realised that he didn't want her not to be around when he returned to his apartment. He wanted her to be there for him and he was irritated with himself for the ridiculous gap in his self-control.

'Because I want to check on my place, make

sure everything's in order. So I'll meet you at the venue. You can text me the details.' She sounded a lot brisker than she felt inside. Inside, she wanted so much more, wanted to take without consequence, just as she wanted to give without thought. She wanted him to love her back and she wanted to shove that feeling into a box and lock it away to protect her fragile heart.

'You'll be nervous.' Lucas raked his fingers through his hair, for once on the back foot with his legendary self-control. 'There'll be reporters there. You won't know what to do. You'll need me to be there with you, by your side.'

Where had that come from?

'But...' His voice as smooth as silk, he regained his footing. 'I see that you might want to check your place and check your mail.' He was back on familiar ground and he relaxed. 'We've got our lives to be getting on with.' He smiled wryly. 'Why kid ourselves otherwise? Don't worry. In a few weeks' time, this will be little more than something you will one day laugh about with your kids.'

'Quite,' Katy responded faintly, sick with heartache, for which she knew that she had only herself to blame. 'I'll see you later.' She forced herself to smile and marvelled that he could be so beautiful, so cool, so composed when she was breaking up inside. But then, he hadn't crossed the lines that she had.

Katy had no idea where to start when it came to looking for something to wear to a black-tie event because she had never been to one in her life before, and certainly, in her wildest imagination, had never dreamt that she would be cast in the starring role at one. She had phoned her mother but, as predicted, it had been impossible at short notice, what with her father's community duties. She had promised that she would send lots of pictures. Now, suddenly, she felt quite alone as she waited for her personal shopper to arrive.

It took over two hours for a dress to be chosen and, no matter how much she told herself that this was all an act, she couldn't help wondering what it would feel like to be trying these clothes on for real, to parade for a man who returned her love, at an event that would celebrate a union that wasn't a charade.

The dress she chose was slim-fitting to the waist, with a back scooped so low that wearing a bra was out of the question, but with an alluringly modest top half that fell in graceful layers to the floor. When she moved, it swirled around her like a cloud, and, staring at the vision looking back in the mirror, she felt the way Cinderella might have felt when the wand had been waved and the rags had been replaced with the ball gown that would later knock Prince Charming off his feet.

Prince Charming, however, had left her thoroughly to her own devices. He was back in the real world and already distancing himself from her without even realising it.

The Fairy Godmother would have to come up with more from her little bag of tricks than ever to turn Lucas into anything more than a guy who had fancied her and had talked her into having sex with him. He would happily sleep with her until the designated time was over, and then he would shove her back into the nearest pumpkin and head straight back to the women he was accustomed to dating, the women who slotted into his lifestyle without causing too many ripples.

She had expected the car from earlier to collect her but when the driver called for her at home, punctual to the last second, and when she went outside, it was to find that a stretch limo was waiting for her.

She felt like a princess. It didn't matter what was real or what was fake, she was floating on a cloud. But that sensation lasted just until they arrived at the hotel and she spotted the hordes of reporters, the beautiful people stopping to smile and pose for photos and the crowds milling around and gaping, as though they were being treated to a live cabaret. The limo pulled to a slow stop and nerves kicked in like a rush of adrenaline injected straight into her blood system. She feared that she wouldn't be able to push her way through the throng of people.

Then, like magic, the crowd parted and she was looking at Lucas as she had never seen him before. Her eyes weren't the only ones on him. As one, everyone turned. He had emerged from the hotel and was impeccably dressed in his white dress shirt and black trousers, everything fitting like a dream. He was so breathtakingly beautiful that Katy could scarcely bring herself to move.

The scene was borderline chaos, with guests arriving, cameras snapping, reporters jostling for prime position, but all of that faded into the background for Lucas as his eyes zeroed in on the open door of the limo and the vision that was Katy stepping out, blinking but holding her own as cameras flashed all around her.

Lucas felt a surge of hot blood rush through him. Of course she was beautiful. He knew that. He had known it from the very first minute he had set eyes on her in his office, but this Katy was a feast for sore eyes, and she held him captive. Their eyes met and he was barely aware of walking towards her, hand outstretched, gently squeezing her small hand as she placed it in his.

'You look amazing, *cara,*' he murmured with gruff honesty.

Nerves threatening to spill over, and frantically aware of the popping of camera bulbs and the rapt attention of people who were so far removed from her world that they could have been from another planet, Katy serenely gazed up at him and smiled in her most confident manner.

'Thank you, and so do you. Shall we go in?'

CHAPTER NINE

KATY HAD TO call upon every ounce of show-manship and self-confidence acquired down the years to deal with the evening.

Blinded by the flash of cameras, which was only slightly more uncomfortable than the in-quisitive eyes of the hundred or so people who had been selectively invited to celebrate the engagement of the year, she held on to Lucas's hand and her fixed, glassy smile didn't waver as she was led like a queen into the hotel.

Lucas had told her that she looked amazing, and that buoyed her up, but her heart was still hammering like a drum beating against her ribcage as she took in the flamboyant décor of the five-star hotel.

It was exquisite. She had no idea how some-thing of this calibre could be rustled up at a moment's notice, but then money could move mountains, and Lucas had oodles of it.

In a daze, she took in the acres of pale marble, the impeccable line of waiting staff in attendance, the dazzling glitter of chandeliers and an informal bar area dominated by an impressive ice sculpture, around which was an even more impressive array of canapés for those who couldn't wait for the waitresses to swing by. There was a buzz of interest and curiosity all around them.

'You'll be fine,' Lucas bent to murmur into her ear. 'After an hour, you'll probably be bored stiff and we'll make our departure.'

'How can we?' Katy queried, genuinely bewildered. 'Aren't *we* the leading actors in the production?'

'I can do whatever I like.' Lucas didn't crack a smile but she could hear the rich amusement in his lowered voice. 'And, if you feel nervous, rest assured that you outshine every other woman here.'

'You're just saying that…they'll all be wondering how on earth you and I have ended up engaged.'

'Then we'd better provide them with an explanation, hadn't we?' He lowered his head and kissed her. His hand was placed protectively on the small of her back and his mouth on hers was warm, fleeting and, oh, so good. Everything and everyone disappeared and Katy surfaced, blinking, ensnared by his dark gaze, her body keening towards his.

She wanted to cling and carry on clinging. Instead, she stroked his cheek briefly with her fingers and then stepped back, recalling the way he had reminded her earlier that what was happening here was just a show.

'Perhaps you could introduce me to the man you're doing the deal with.' She smiled, looking around her and doing her best to blank out the sea of beautiful faces. 'And thanks,' she added in a low voice, while her body continued to sizzle in the aftermath of that kiss. 'That was an inspired way to provide an explanation. I think you're going to be far better at this than I could ever hope to be.'

'I'll take that as a compliment,' Lucas drawled, wanting nothing more than to escort her right back into his limo and take her to his bed. 'Although I'm not entirely sure whether it was meant to be. Now, shall we get this party started?'

Having been introduced to Ken Huang, who was there with his family and two men who looked very much like bodyguards, Katy gradually edged away from the protective zone around Lucas.

Curiosity warred with nerves and won. She was surrounded by the beautiful people you saw in the gossip magazines and, after a while, she found that she was actually enjoying the experience of talking to some of those famous faces, discovering that they were either more normal than she had thought or far less so.

Every so often she would find herself drifting back towards Lucas but, even when she wasn't by his side, she was very much aware of his dark gaze on her, following her movements, and that made her tingle all over. There was something wonderfully possessive about that gaze and she had to constantly stop herself from luxuriating in the fallacy that it was heartfelt rather than a deliberate show of what was expected from a man supposedly in love with the woman wearing his ring.

Katy longed to glue herself to his side but she knew that circulating would not only remind Lucas that she was independent and happy to get on with the business of putting on a good show for the assembled crowd, just as he was, but would also shore up the barriers she knew she should mentally be erecting between them.

Everything had been so straightforward when she had been living with the illusion that what she felt for him was desire and nothing more.

With that illusion stripped away, she felt achingly vulnerable, and more than once she wondered how she was going to hold on to this so-called relationship for the period of time they had allotted to it.

In theory, she would have her window, during which she could allow herself to really enjoy him, even if she knew that her enjoyment was going to be short-lived.

In practice, she was already quailing at the prospect of walking away from him. He would probably pat her on the back and tell her that they could remain good friends. The truth was that she wasn't built to live in the moment, to heck with what happened next. Investing in a future was a by-product of her upbringing and, even though she could admit to the down side of that approach, she still feverishly wondered whether she would be able to adopt the right attitude, an attitude that would allow her to live from one moment to the next.

Thoughts buzzing in her head like a horde of hornets released from their nest, she swirled the champagne in her glass and stared down at the golden liquid while she pictured that last conversation between them. She dearly wished that she had the experience and the temperament to enjoy what she had now, instead of succumbing to dark thoughts about a future that was never going to be.

From across the crowded room, Lucas found his fiancée with the unerring accuracy of a heat-seeking missile. No matter where she was, he seemed to possess the uncanny ability to locate her. She wasn't taller than everyone else, and her outfit didn't stand out as being materially different from every other fancy long, designer dress, but somehow she emanated a light that beckoned to him from wherever she was. It was as if he was tuned into her on a wave length that was inaudible to everyone except him.

Right now, and for the first time that evening, she was on her own, thoughtfully staring down into a flute of champagne as though looking for answers to something in the liquid.

Abruptly bringing his conversation with two

top financiers to an end, Lucas weaved his way towards her, approaching her from behind.

'You're thinking,' he murmured, leaning down so that he could whisper into her ear.

Katy started and spun round, and her heart began to beat faster. *Thud, thud, thud.*

She had shyly told the three colleagues who'd been invited to the ball about Lucas, glossing over how they had met and focusing instead on how they had been irresistibly drawn towards one another.

'You know how it is,' she had laughed coquettishly, knowing that she was telling nothing but the absolute truth, 'Sometimes you get hit by something and, before you know it, you're going along for the ride and nothing else matters.'

Lucas's stunning eyes on her now really did make her feel as though she had been hit head-on by a speeding train and she had to look down just in case he caught the ghost of an expression that might alert him to the way she really felt about him.

'Tired?' Lucas asked, drawing her towards the dance floor.

A jazz band had been playing for the past forty-five minutes, the music forming a perfect backdrop to the sound of voices and laughter. The musicians were on a podium, in classic coat and tails, and they very much looked as though they had stepped straight out of a twenties movie set.

'A little,' Katy admitted. His fingers were linked through hers and his thumb was absently stroking the side of hers. It made her whole body feel hot and she was conscious of her bare nipples rubbing against the silky fabric of her dress. The tips were stiff and sensitive and, the more his thumb idly stroked hers, the more her body went into melt down.

This was what he did to her and she knew that if she had any sense at all she would enjoy it while she had it. Instead of tormenting herself with thoughts of what life would be like when he disappeared from it, she should be relishing the prospect of climbing into bed with him later and making love until she was too exhausted to move a muscle.

'It's really tiring talking to loads of people you don't know,' she added breathlessly as he drew her to the side of the dance floor and turned her to face him.

The lighting had been dimmed and his gorgeous face was all shadows and angles.

'But you've been doing a pretty good job of it,' Lucas assured her with a wry smile. 'And here I was imagining that you would be a little out of your depth.'

Katy laughed, eyes dancing as she looked up at him. 'That must have been a blessed relief for you.'

'What makes you say that?' After spending the past hour or so doing the rounds, Lucas felt relaxed for the first time that evening. No one had dared ask him any direct questions about the engagement that had sprung from nowhere, and he had not enlightened anyone, aside from offering a measured explanation to Ken Huang and his wife, both of whom, he had been amused to note, were full of praise for the romance of the situation. He had thought them far too contained for flowery congratulations but he'd been wrong on that point.

Under normal circumstances, he would have used the time to talk business. There were a number of influential financiers there, as well as several political figures with whom interesting conversations could have been initiated. However, his attention had been far too taken up with Katy and following her progress through the room.

People were keen to talk to her; he had no idea what she'd told them, but whatever it was, she had obviously struck the right note.

With women and men alike. Indeed, he hadn't failed to notice that some of the men had seemed a lot busier sizing her up than listening to whatever she had had to say. From a distance, Lucas had had to swallow down the urge to muscle in on the scene and claim his property—because she wasn't his and that was exactly how it ought to be. Possessiveness was a trait he had no time for and he refused to allow it to enter into the arrangement they had between them.

But several times he had felt his jaw tighten at the way her personal space had been invaded by men who probably had wives or girlfriends somewhere in the room, creeps with fancy jobs and flash cars who figured that they could do what they wanted with whomever they chose. Arrangement or no arrangement, Lucas had been quite prepared to land a punch if need be, but he knew that not a single man in the room would dare cross him by overstepping the mark.

Still.

Had she even noticed the over-familiar-ity of some of those guys? Should he have warned her that she might encounter the sort of men who made her odious ex pale in comparison?

'I can't imagine you would have wanted to spend the evening holding my hand,' she teased with a catch in her voice. 'That kiss of yours did the trick, and I have to say no one expressed any doubt about the fact that the most unlikely two people in the world decided to get engaged.'

'Even the men who had their eyes on stalks when they were talking to you?'

Katy looked at him, startled. 'What on earth are you talking about?'

'Forget it,' Lucas muttered gruffly, flushing.

'Are you *jealous*?'

'I'm not the jealous type.' He downed his whisky in one long swallow and dumped the empty glass, along with her champagne flute, on a tray carried by one of the glamorous waitresses who seemed to know just where to be at the right time to relieve important guests of their empty glasses.

'No.' Katy was forced to agree because he really wasn't, and anyway, jealousy was the domain of the person who actually *felt* something. She smiled but it was strained. 'No need to point out the obvious!'

Lucas frowned even though she was actually saying all the right things. 'That kiss, by the way,' he murmured, shifting his hand to cup the nape of her neck, keen to get off a subject that was going nowhere, 'Wasn't just about making the right impression.'

'It wasn't?'

'Have you stopped to consider that I might actually have wanted to kiss you?'

Katy blushed and said with genuine honesty, 'I thought it was more of a tactical gesture.'

'Then you obviously underestimated the impact of your dress,' Lucas delivered huskily. 'When I saw you get out of the back of my limo, my basic instinct was to get in with you, slam the door and get my driver to take us back to my apartment.'

'I don't think your guests would have been too impressed.' But every word sent a powerful charge of awareness racing through her already heated body. He was just talking about sex, she told herself weakly. Okay, so he was looking at her as though she was a feast for the eyes, but that had nothing to do with anything other than desire.

Lucas was excellent when it came to sex. He was just lousy when it came to emotion. Not only was he uninterested in exploring anything at all beyond the physical, but he was proud of his control in that arena. If he had foresworn involvement on an emotional level because of one bad experience with a woman, then Katy knew that somehow she would have tried to find a way of making herself indispensable to him. A bad experience left scars, just as Duncan had left her with scars, but scars healed over, because time moved on and one poor experience would always end up buried under layers of day-to-day life.

But Lucas wasn't like that. He wasn't a guy who had had one bad experience but was essentially still interested in having a meaningful relationship with a woman. He wasn't a guy who, even deep down, had faith in the power of love.

Lucas's cynicism stemmed from a darker place and it had been formed at so young an age that it was now an embedded part of his personality.

'Do I look like the kind of man who lives his life to impress other people?' he asked, libido kicking fast into gear as his eyes drifted down to her breasts. Knowing what those breasts looked like and tasted like added to the pulsing ache in his groin. 'Quite honestly, I can't think of anything I'd rather do than leave this room right now and head back to my apartment. Failing that, rent a bloody room in the hotel and use it for an hour.'

'That would be rude.' But her eyes were slumberous as she looked at him from under her lashes. 'We should dance instead.'

'You think that dancing is a good substitute for having mind-blowing sex?'

'Stop that!' She pulled him onto the dance floor. The music's tempo had slowed and the couples who were dancing in the half-light were entwined with one another.

It was almost midnight. Where on earth had the time gone? Lucas pulled Katy onto the dance floor and then held her so close to him that she could feel the steady beat of his heart and the pressure of his body, warm and so, so tempting.

She rested her head on his chest and he curled his fingers into her hair and leant into her.

This was heaven. For the duration of this dance, with his arms around her, she could forget that she wasn't living the dream.

Lucas looked down and saw the glitter of the diamond on her finger. The ring had fitted her perfectly, no need to be altered. He had slipped it onto her finger and it had belonged there.

Except, it didn't. Did it?

They had started something in full knowledge of how and when it would end. Katy had proposed a course of action that had been beneficial to them both and at the time, which was only a matter of days ago, Lucas had admired the utter practicality of the proposal.

She had assured him that involvement was not an issue for either of them because they were little more than two people from different planets who had collided because of the peculiar circumstances that had hurled them into the same orbit.

They had an arrangement and it was an arrangement that both of them had under control.

Except, was it?

Lucas didn't want to give house room to doubt, but that ring quietly glittering on her finger was posing questions that left him feeling uneasy and a little panicked, if truth be known.

The song came to an end and he drew away from her.

'We should go and say goodbye to Huang and his family. I've spotted them out of the corner of my eye and they've gathered by the exit. Mission accomplished, I think.'

Katy blinked, abruptly yanked out of the pleasant little cloud in which she had been nestled.

For all that common sense was telling her to be wary of this beautiful man who had stolen her heart like a thief in the night, her heart was rebelling at every practical step forward she tried to take.

She should pull back, yet here she was, wanting nothing more than to linger in his arms and for the music to never end.

She should remember Duncan and the hurt he had caused because, however upset she had been—and she now realised it had been on the mild end of the scale—whatever she had thought at the time, it would be nothing compared to what she would suffer when Lucas walked away from her. But nothing could have been less important in that moment than her cheating ex. In fact, she could barely remember what he looked like, and it had been that way for ages.

She had weeks of this farce to go through!

She should steel herself against her own cowardly emotions and do what her head was telling her made sense—which was appreciate him while she could; which was gorge herself on everything he had to offer and look for no more than that.

But her own silly romanticism undermined her at every turn.

She gazed up at him helplessly. 'Mission accomplished?'

'We did what we set out to do,' Lucas said flatly. 'You only spent a short while with Ken Huang and his family, but let me tell you that he was charmed by our tale of love at first sight.'

'Oh, good.' He had already turned away and she followed him, hearing herself say all the right things to the businessman while sifting through her conflicting emotions to try and find a path she could follow. In a show of unity, Lucas had his arm around her waist lovingly, and she could see how thrilled Ken Huang and his wife were by the romance.

Mission accomplished, indeed.

'Time to go, I think.' Lucas turned to her the second Huang had departed.

'Where?'

'Where do you think? We're engaged, Katy. Getting my driver to deliver you back to your flat is a sure-fire way of getting loose tongues wagging.'

'We're going back to your place?'

'Unless you have a better idea?' He shot her a wolfish smile but this time her blood didn't sizzle as it would have normally. This time she didn't give that soft, yielding sigh as her body took over and her ability to think disappeared like water down a plughole.

Mission accomplished. It was back to business for Lucas, and for that read 'sex'. They would go to his apartment, like the madly in love couple they weren't, and he would take her to his bed and do what he did so very, very well. He would send her pliant body into the stratosphere but would leave her heart untouched.

'We need to talk.' Nerves poured through her. She couldn't do this. She'd admitted how she felt about Lucas to herself and now she couldn't see a way of continuing what they had, pretending that nothing had changed.

'What about?'

'Us,' Katy told him quietly, and Lucas stilled. 'Follow me.'

'Where are we going? I mean, I'd rather not have this conversation in your apartment.'

'I'm on nodding acquaintance with the manager of this hotel. I will ensure we have privacy for whatever it is you feel you need to talk about.'

The shutters had dropped. Katy could feel it in his body language. Gone was the easy warmth and the sexy teasing. She followed him away from the ball room, leaving behind the remaining guests. He had said his goodbyes to the people who mattered and, where she would have at least tried to circulate and make some polite noises before leaving, Lucas had no such concerns.

She hung back as he had a word with the manager, who appeared from nowhere, as though his entire evening had been spent waiting to see if there was anything he could do for Lucas. There was and he did it, leading them to a quiet seating area and assuring them that they would have perfect privacy.

'Will I need something stiff for this *talk*?' Lucas asked once the door was closed quietly behind them. On the antique desk by the open fireplace, there was an assortment of drinks, along with glasses and an ice bucket. Without waiting for an answer, he helped himself to a whisky and then remained where he was, perched against the desk, his dark eyes resting on her without any expression at all.

Katy gazed helplessly at him for a few seconds then took a deep, steadying breath.

'I can't do this.' She hadn't thought out what she was going to say but, now the words had left her mouth, she felt very calm.

'You can't do what?'

'This. *Us.*' She spread her arms wide in a gesture of frustration. His lack of expression was like an invisible force field between them and it added strength to the decision she had taken impulsively to tell him how she felt.

'This is as far as I can go,' she told him quietly. 'I've done the public appearance thing and I've had the photos taken and I...I can't continue this charade for any longer. I can't pretend that...that...'

Lucas wasn't going to help her out. He knew what she was saying, he knew why she was saying it and he also knew that it was something he had recognised over time but had chosen to ignore because it suited him.

'You love me.'

Those three words dropped like stones into

still water, sending out ripples that grew bigger and bigger until they filled the space between them.

Stressed out, stricken and totally unable to tell an outright lie, Katy stared at him, her face white, her arms folded.

'I wish I could tell you that that wasn't true, but I can't. I'm sorry.'

'You knew how I felt about commitment...'

'Yes, I knew! But sometimes the heart doesn't manage to listen to the head!'

'I told you I wasn't in the market for love and commitment.' He recalled what he had felt when he had seen other men looking at her and then later, when his gaze had dropped to that perfect diamond on her finger, and something close to fear gripped him. 'I will *never* love you the way you want to be loved and the way you deserve to be loved, *cara*. I can desire you but I am incapable of anything more.'

'Surely you can't say that?' she heard herself plead in a low, driven voice, hating herself, because she should have had a bit more pride.

Lucas's mouth twisted. In the midst of heightened emotions, he could still grudgingly appreciate her bravery in having a conversation that was only ever going to go in a preordained direction. But then she *was* brave, wasn't she? In the way she always spoke her mind, the way she would dig her heels in and defend what she believed in even if he was giving her a hard time. In the way she acted, as she had at an event which would have stretched her to the limits and taken her far out of her comfort zone.

'I can't feel the way you do,' Lucas said, turning away from her wide, green, honest eyes and feeling a cad. But it wasn't his fault that he just couldn't give her what she wanted, and it was better for him to be upfront about that right now!

And maybe this was a positive outcome. What would the alternative have been—that a charade born of necessity dragged on and on until he was forced to prise her away from him? She had taken the bull by the horns and was doing the walking away herself. She was rescuing him from an awkward situation and he wondered why he wasn't feeling better about that.

He hated 'clingy' and he didn't do 'needy' and a woman who was bold enough to declare her love was both. He should be feeling relieved!

'I've seen how destructive love can be,' he told her harshly. 'And I've sworn to myself that I would never allow it to enter my life, never allow it to destroy me.' He held up one hand, as though she had interrupted him in mid-flow when in fact she hadn't said a word. 'You're going to tell me that you can change me. I can't change. This is who I am—a man with far too many limitations for someone as romantic and idealistic as you.'

'I realise that,' Katy told him simply. 'I'm not asking you to change.'

Suddenly restless, Lucas pushed himself away from the desk to pace the room. He felt caged and trapped—two very good indications that this was a situation that should be ended without delay because, for a man who valued the freedom of having complete control over his life, *caged and trapped* didn't work.

'You'll meet someone…who can give you what you want and need,' he rasped, his normally graceful movements jerky as he continued to pace the room, only stopping now and again to look at her where she had remained standing as still as a statue. 'And of course, you'll be compensated,' he told her gruffly.

'I'm not following you.'

'Compensated. For what you've done. I'll make sure that you have enough money so that you can build your life wherever you see fit. Rest assured that you will never want for anything. You will be able to buy any house you want in any part of London, and naturally I will ensure that you have enough of a comfort blanket financially so that you need not rush to find another job. In fact, you will be able to teach full-time, and you won't have to worry about finding something alongside the teaching because you won't have to pay rent.'

'You're offering me money,' Katy said numbly, frozen to the spot and stripped bare of all her defences. Had he any idea how humiliating this was for her—to be told that she would be *paid off* for services rendered? She wanted the ground to open up and swallow her. She was still wearing the princess dress but she could have been clothed in rags because she certainly didn't feel like Cinderella at the ball.

'I want to make sure that you're all right at the end of this,' Lucas murmured huskily, dimly unsettled by her lack of expression and the fact that she didn't seem to hear what he was saying. The colour had drained from her face. Her hair, in contrast, was shockingly vibrant, hanging over her shoulders in a torrent of silken copper.

'And of course, you can keep the ring,' he continued in the lengthening silence. 'In fact, I insist you do.'

'As a reminder?' Katy asked quietly. 'Of the good old days?'

The muscles in her legs finally remembered how to function and she walked towards him stiffly.

For one crazy, wild moment, Lucas envisaged her arms around him, but the moment didn't last long, because she paused to meet his eyes squarely and directly.

'Oh, Lucas. I don't want your money.' She felt the engagement ring with her finger, enjoying the forbidden thought of what it would feel like for the ring to be hers for real, and then she gently pulled it off her finger and held it out towards him. 'And I don't want your ring either.'

Then she turned and left the room, noiselessly shutting the door behind her.

CHAPTER TEN

BEHIND THE WHEEL of his black sports car, Lucas was forced to cut his speed and to slow down to accommodate the network of winding roads that circled the village where Katy's parents lived like a complex spider's web.

Since leaving the motorway, where he had rediscovered the freedom of not being driven by someone else, he had found himself surrounded on all sides by the alien landscape of rural Britain.

He should be somewhere else. In fact, he should be on the other side of the world. Instead, however, he had sent his next in command to do the honours and finalise work on the deal that had been a game changer.

Lucas didn't know when or how the thing he had spent the better part of a year and a half consolidating had faded into insignificance. He just knew that two days ago Katy had walked out of his life and, from that moment on, the deal that had once upon a long time ago commandeered all his attention no longer mattered.

The only thing that had mattered was the driving need to get her back and, for two days, he had fought that need with every tool at his disposal. For two days, Lucas had told himself that Katy was the very epitome of what he had spent a lifetime avoiding. She lived and breathed a belief in a romantic ideal that he had always scorned. Despite her poor experience, she nurtured a faith in love that should have been buried under the weight of disappointment. She was the sort of woman who terrified men like him.

And, more than all of that put together, she had come right out and spoken words that she surely must have known would be taboo for him.

After everything he had told her.

She had fallen in love with him. She had blatantly ignored all the 'do not trespass' signs he had erected around himself and fallen in love with him. He should have been thankful that she had not wept and begged him to return her love. He should have been grateful that, as soon as she had made that announcement, she had removed the engagement ring and handed it back to him.

He should have thanked his lucky stars that she had then proceeded to exit his life without any fuss or fanfare.

There would be a little untidiness when it came to the engagement that had lasted five seconds before imploding, and the press would have a field day for a week or so, but that hadn't bothered him. Ken Huang would doubtless be disappointed, but he would already be moving on to enjoy his family life without the stress of a company he had been keen to sell to the right bidder, and would not lose sleep over it because it was a done deal.

Life as Lucas knew it could be returned to its state of normality.

Everything was positive, but Katy had left him and, stubborn, blind idiot that he was, it was only when that door had shut behind her that he had realised how much of his heart she was taking with her.

He had spent two days trying to convince himself that he shouldn't follow her, before caving in, because he just hadn't been able to envisage life without her in it, at which point he had abandoned all hope of being able to control his destiny. Along with his heart, that was something else she had taken with her.

And now here he was, desperately hoping that he hadn't left everything too late.

His satnav was telling him to veer off onto a country lane that promised a dead end, but he obeyed the instructions and, five minutes later, with the sun fading fast, the vicarage she had told him about came into view, as picturesque as something lifted from the lid of a box of chocolates.

Wisteria clambered over faded yellow stone. The vicarage was a solid, substantial building behind which stretched endless acres of fields, on which grazing sheep were blobs of white, barely moving against the backdrop of a pink-and-orange twilit sky. The drive leading to the vicarage was long, straight and bordered by neat lawns and flower beds that had obviously taken thought in the planting stage.

For the first time in his life, Lucas was in a position of not knowing what would happen next. He'd never had to beg for anyone before and he felt that he might have to beg now. He wondered whether she had decided that replacing him immediately would be a cure for the pain of confessing her love to a guy who had sent her on her way with the very considerate offer of financial compensation for any inconvenience. When Lucas thought about the way he had responded to her, he shuddered in horror.

He honestly wouldn't blame her if she refused to set eyes on him.

He drove slowly up the drive and curled his car to the side of the vicarage, then killed the engine, quietly opened the door and got out.

'Darling, will you get that?'

Propped in front of the newspaper where she had been scouring ads for local jobs for the past hour and a half, Katy looked up. Sarah Brennan was at the range stirring something. Conversation was thin on the ground because her parents were both so busy tiptoeing around her, making sure they didn't say the wrong thing.

Her father was sitting opposite her with a glass of wine in his hand, and every so often Katy would purposefully ignore the look of concern he gave her, because he was worried about her.

She had shown up, burst into tears and confessed everything. She had wanted lots of tea and sympathy, and she had got it from her parents, who had put on a brave face and said all the right things about time being a great healer, rainbows round corners and silver linings on clouds, but they had been distraught on her behalf. She had seen it in the worried looks they gave one another when they didn't think she was looking, and it was there in the silences, where before there would have been lots and lots of chat and laughter.

'I should have known better,' Katy had conceded the evening before when she had finally stopped crying. 'He was very honest. He wasn't into marriage, and the engagement was just something that served a purpose.'

'To spare us thinking you were…were…' Her mother had stumbled as she had tried to find a polite way of saying *easy*. 'Do you honestly think we would have thought that, when we know you so very well, my darling?'

Katy could have told them that sparing them had only been part of the story. The other part had been her concern for Lucas's reputation. Even then, she must have been madly in love with him, because she had cared more about his reputation than he had.

She also didn't mention the money he had offered her. She felt cheapened just thinking about that and her parents would have been horrified. Even with Lucas firmly behind her, she still loved him so much that she couldn't bear to have her parents drill that final nail in his coffin.

The doorbell rang again and Katy blinked, focused and realised that her mother was looking at her oddly, waiting for her actually to do something about getting the door.

Her father was already rising to his feet and Katy waved him down with an apologetic smile. She wondered who would be calling at this time but then, for a small place it was remarkably full of people who urgently needed to talk to her parents about something or other. Just as soon as the cat was out of the bag, the hot topic of conversation would actually be *her*, and she grimaced when she thought about that.

She was distracted as she opened the door. The biggest bunch of red roses was staring her in the face. Someone would have to have wreaked havoc in a rose garden to have gathered so many. Katy stared down, mind blank, her thoughts only beginning to sift through possibilities and come up with the right answer when she noted the expensive leather shoes.

Face drained of colour, she raised her eyes

slowly, and there he was, the man whose image had not been out of her head for the past two agonising days since they had gone their separate ways.

'Can I come in?' Unfamiliar nerves turned the question into an aggressive statement of fact. Lucas wasn't sure whether flowers were the right gesture. Should he have gone for something more substantial? But then, Katy hated ostentatious displays of wealth. Uncertainty gripped him, and he was so unfamiliar with the sensation that he barely recognised it for what it was.

'What are you doing here?' Katy was too shocked to expand on that but she folded her arms, stiffened her spine and recollected what it had felt like when he had offered to pay her off. That was enough to ignite her anger, and she planted herself squarely in front of him, because there was no way she was going to let him into the house.

'I've come to see you.'

'What for?' she asked coldly.

'Please let me in, Katy. I don't want to have this conversation with you on your doorstep.'

'My parents are inside.'

'Yes, I thought they might be here.'

'Why have you come here, Lucas? We have nothing to say to one another. I don't want your flowers. I don't want you coming into this house and I don't want you meeting my parents. I've told them everything, and now I just want to get on with my life and pretend that I never met you.'

'You don't mean that.'

'Yes. I do.'

Her voice was cold and composed but she was a mess inside. She badly wanted her body to do what her brain was urgently telling it to do, but like a runaway train it was veering out of control, responding to him with frightening ferocity. More than anything in the world, she wanted to creep into his arms, rest her head against his chest and pretend that her life wasn't cracking up underneath her; she hated herself for that weakness and hated him for showing up and exposing her to it.

She glanced anxiously over her shoulder. In a minute, she knew her father would probably appear behind her, curious as to who had rung the doorbell. Lucas followed her gaze and knew exactly what she was thinking. He was here and he was going to say what he had come to say and, if forcing his way in and flagrantly taking advantage of the fact that she wouldn't be able to do a thing about it because it would create a scene in front of her parents was what it took, then so be it.

What was the point of an opportunity presenting itself if you didn't take advantage of it?

So he did just that. Hand flat against the door, he stepped forward and pushed it open and, caught unawares, Katy fell back with a look that was part surprise, part horror and part incandescent rage.

'I need to talk to you, Katy. I need you to listen to me.'

'And you think that gives you the right to barge into my house?'

'If it's the only way of getting you to listen to me...'

'I told you, I'm not interested in anything you have to say, and if you think that you can sweet talk your way back into my bed then you can forget it!' Her voice was a low, angry hiss and her colour was high.

His body was so familiar to her that she was responding to him like an engine that had been turned on and was idling, ready to accelerate.

From behind, Katy heard her mother calling out to her and she furiously stepped aside as

Lucas entered the house, *her sanctuary,* with his blasted red roses, on a mission to wreck her life all over again. No way was she going to allow her parents to think that a bunch of flowers meant anything, and she took them from him and unceremoniously dumped them in an umbrella stand that was empty of umbrellas.

'I should have bought you the sports car,' Lucas murmured and Katy glared at him. 'That wouldn't have fitted into an umbrella stand.'

'You wouldn't have dared.'

'When it comes to getting what I want, there's nothing I won't do.'

Katy didn't have the opportunity to rebut that contentious statement because her mother appeared, and then shortly after her father, and there they stood in the doorway of the kitchen, mouths round with surprise, eyes like saucers and brains conjuring up heaven only knew what. Katy shuddered to think.

And, if she had anticipated Lucas being on the back foot, the wretched man managed, in the space of forty-five minutes, to achieve the impossible.

After *everything* she had told her parents— after she had filled them in on her hopeless

situation, told them that she was in love with
a man who could never return her love, a man
whose only loyal companion would ever be his
work—she seethed and fumed from the side-
lines as her parents were won over by a display
of charm worthy of an acting award.

Why had Lucas come? Shouldn't he have
been in China working on the deal that had
ended up changing *her* life more than it had
changed his?

He didn't love her and, by a process of common sense and elimination, she worked out the
only thing that could possibly have brought
him to her parents' house would be an offer to
continue their fling. Lucas was motivated by
sex, so sex had to be the reason he was here.

The more Katy thought about that, the an-
grier she became, and by the time her parents
began making noises about going out for supper so that she and Lucas could talk she was
fit to explode.

'How *dare* you?' That was the first thing she
said as soon as they were on their own in the
comfortable sitting room, with its worn flow-
ered sofas, framed family photos on the man-
telpiece and low coffee table groaning under
the weight of the magazines her mother was

addicted to. 'How *dare you* waltz into my life here and try and *take over*? Do you think for a moment that if you manage to get to my parents that you'll get to me as well?'

She was standing on the opposite side of the room to him, her arms folded, the blood running hot in her veins as she tried her hardest not to be moved by the dark, sinful beauty that could get to her every time.

It infuriated her that he could just *stand there*, watching her with eyes that cloaked his thoughts, leaning indolently against the wall and not saying anything, which had the effect of propelling her into hysterical, attacking speech. She was being precisely the sort of person she didn't want to be. If she wasn't careful, she would start throwing things in a minute, and she definitely wasn't going to sink to that level.

Lucas watched her and genuinely wasn't sure how to proceed. Where did you start when it came to talking about feelings? He didn't know because he'd never been there before. But she was furious, and he didn't blame her, and standing in silence wasn't going to progress anything.

'I really like your parents,' Lucas said, a pro-

pos of nothing, and she glared at him as though
he had taken leave of his senses.

'You've wasted your time,' she told him
flatly. 'I'm not interested in having another
fling with you, Lucas. I don't care whether
my parents fell in love with you. I want you to
leave and I don't want to see you ever again.
I just want to be left in peace to get on with
my life.'

'How can you get on with your life when
you're in love with me?'

Mortification and anger coursed through
her, because just like that he had cut her down
at the knees. He had taken her confession and
used it against her.

'How can *I* get on with my life when I'm
in love with *you*?' Lucas realised that he was
perspiring. Sealing multi-million-pound deals
were a walk in the park compared to this.

Thrown into instant confusion, Katy gaped,
unwilling to believe him. If he'd loved her, he
wouldn't have let her go, she thought painfully.
He would have tried to stop her. He wouldn't
have offered her money to compensate for all
the other things he couldn't provide.

Lucas noted the rampant disbelief on her
face, and again he couldn't blame her.

'You don't believe me and I understand that.' His voice was unsteady and he raked his fingers through his hair in an unusually clumsy gesture. 'I'd made it clear that I could never be interested in having the sort of relationship I knew you wanted. You were so...so *different* that I couldn't get my head around ever falling for you. I'll be honest—I could never get my head around falling for *anyone*. I'd always equated love with vulnerability, and vulnerability with being hurt.'

'Why are you telling me this?' Katy cried jerkily. 'Don't you think I don't know all that?' But the uncertainty on his face was throwing her off-balance, and hope was unfurling and blossoming fast, yanking the ground from under her feet and setting up a drumbeat inside her that was stronger than all the caution she was desperate to impose on herself.

'What you *don't* know is that you came along and everything changed for me. You made me feel...different. When I was around you, life was in Technicolor. I put it down to the incredible sex. I put it down to the fact that I was in a state of suspended animation, far from the daily demands of my office. I never put it down to the truth, which was that I was falling for you. I was blind, but then I'd never expected to fall in love. Not with you, not with any woman.'

'You mean it? Please don't say anything you don't mean. I couldn't bear it.' Was this some ploy to try and talk her into bed? He was right, the sex *had* been incredible. Was he working up to an encore by flattering her? But, when she looked at him, the discomfort on his face was palpable and it made her breathing shallow and laborious.

'You confused me. There were times when I felt disorientated, as though the world had suddenly been turned upside down, and when that happened I just told myself that it was because you were a novelty, nothing like what I was used to. But I behaved differently when I was around you. You made me say things I've never said to anyone else and I felt comfortable doing it.'

'But you didn't try and stop me,' Katy whispered. 'I told you how I felt and you...you let me walk away. No, worse than that, you offered me money.'

'Please don't remind me,' Lucas said quietly. Somehow, he had closed the gap between them, but he was still hesitant to reach out and touch her even though he badly wanted to do just that.

'You have to understand that money is the currency I'm familiar with, not love. My father was derailed after my mother's death. I grew up watching him get carried along on emotional riptides that stripped him of his ability to function, and that taught me about the importance of self-control and the need to focus on things that were constant. Relationships, in my head, were associated with frightening inconsistency and I wanted no part of that. The only relationship I would ever consider would be one that didn't impact on the quality of my life. A relationship with a woman who wanted the same sort of thing that I did.' He smiled wryly. 'Not an emotional, outspoken and utterly adorable firebrand like you.'

Katy liked all of those descriptions. She liked the expression on his face even more, and just like that her caution faded away and her heart leapt and danced and made her want to grin stupidly at him.

'Keep talking,' she whispered, and he raised his eyebrows and smiled at her.

'So here I am,' Lucas said simply. 'I'd worked like the devil for a deal that, in the end, won't mean anything if you aren't by my side. I think that was when I was forced to accept that the only thing that mattered to me was *you*. I should have guessed when I realised how protective you made me feel and how possessive. You make me the best person I could be, and that means someone who can be hurt, who has feelings, who's willing to wear his heart on his sleeve.' He pulled her towards him and Katy sighed as she was enveloped in a hug that was so fierce that she could feel the beating of his heart. He curled his fingers into her hair and tilted her face to deliver a gentle kiss on her lips.

'I never expected to fall in love with you either,' she admitted softly. 'I was so certain that I knew the sort of guy I should end up with, and it wasn't a guy like you. But it's like you fill in the missing pieces of me and make me complete. It's weird, but when I met Duncan I was looking for love, looking for that *something else*, but I wasn't looking for anything at all when I met you—yet love found me.'

'I know what you mean. I was comfortable *wanting* you because I understood the dynamics of desire. Strangely, loving you has made me understand how my father ended up becoming entangled in a series of inappropriate relationships. He was deeply in love with my mother and he wanted to replicate that. Before I met you, I just didn't get it, but then I never understood how powerful love could be and how it can turn a black-and-white life into something filled with colour and light.'

'And when I returned home,' Katy admitted, 'And I saw the interaction between my parents, I knew that I could never settle for anything less than what they have. I was so upset when you showed up because I thought you'd come to try and persuade me into carrying on with what we had. Maybe because of the deal, or maybe because you still fancied me, even though you didn't love me.'

'Now you know the real reason I turned up with those flowers that you dumped out of sight—you want the fairy-tale romance and I want to be the lucky person who gives it to you. Will you do me the honour of marrying me, my darling? For real and for ever?'

'Just try and stop me...'

EPILOGUE

KATY PAUSED AND looked at Lucas, who was standing staring out to the sea, half-naked because he enjoyed swimming at night, something he had yet to convince her to try.

There was a full moon and the light threw his magnificent body into shadow. To think that a little over a year ago she had come aboard this very yacht, kicking and screaming and accusing him of kidnapping her.

She smiled because that felt like a lifetime ago and so much had happened since then. The engagement that wasn't an engagement had turned into the real thing and they had been married, not once, but *twice*. There was a lavish affair, held a week after the actual wedding, where reporters had jostled for prime position and celebrities had emerged from limos dressed to kill for the event of the century. But first had come something altogether smaller, in her home village, where they had married at a ceremony officiated by her father at the picturesque local church. The reception there had been warm, small and cosy.

Lavish or cosy, Katy just knew that she was the happiest person in the world.

They had had their honeymoon in Italy, where they had stayed with Lucas's father for a few days. Katy knew that she would be seeing a great deal more of Marco Cipriani, because he had got along with her parents like a house on fire, and plans were already afoot for him to discover the joys of the northern countryside at its finest at Christmas.

And she knew that during the festive season there would certainly be reason for a great deal of celebration.

'Lucas...'

Lucas turned, and his heart stopped just for a second as he watched the woman who had so taken over his life that contemplating an existence without her was unthinkable. He smiled, held his hand out and watched her walk towards him, glorious in a casual, long dress which he knew he would be removing later.

Katy walked straight into his open arms and then looked up at him with a smile. 'I have something to say… We both have eight months to start thinking of some names…'

'Names?'

'For our baby, my darling. I'm pregnant.' She tiptoed to plant a kiss on his very sexy mouth.

'My darling, perfect wife.' Lucas closed his eyes and allowed himself to be swept away in the moment before looking down at her with love. 'I never thought that life could get any better, but I do believe it has…'

* * * * *

If you enjoyed
CIPRIANI'S INNOCENT CAPTIVE,
why not explore these other
Cathy Williams stories?

THE SECRET SANCHEZ HEIR
BOUGHT TO WEAR THE
BILLIONAIRE'S RING
SNOWBOUND WITH HIS INNOCENT
TEMPTATION
A VIRGIN FOR VASQUEZ
SEDUCED INTO HER BOSS'S SERVICE
Available now!

Get 2 Free Books,
Plus 2 Free Gifts—
just for trying the Reader Service!

⟡ HARLEQUIN
INTRIGUE